WINTER QUARTERS

by Osvaldo Soriano and available
from Readers International:

A Funny Dirty Little War

OSVALDO SORIANO

WINTER
QUARTERS
A Novel of Argentina

translated by Nick Caistor

readers international

The title of this book in Spanish is *Cuarteles de invierno,*
first published in 1982 by Editorial Bruguera, Barcelona.
© Osvaldo Soriano 1982

First published in English by Readers International Inc,
Columbia, Louisiana and Readers International, London.
Editorial inquiries to the London office at 8 Strathray
Gardens, London NW3 4NY, England. US/Canadian
inquiries to the Subscriber Service Department,
P.O. Box 959, Columbia LA 71418-0959 USA.

Translation © Readers International Inc 1989
All rights reserved

Cover illustration and design by
the Argentinian artist Oscar Zarate
Printed and bound in Malta by Interprint Limited

Library of Congress Catalog Card Number: 89-61873

British Library Cataloguing in Publication Data
Soriano, Osvaldo, *1943-*
    Winter Quarters: a novel of Argentina.
    I. Title   II. Cuarteles de invierno. *English*
    863

ISBN 0-930523-69-5 Hardcover
ISBN 0-930523-70-9 Paperback

WINTER QUARTERS

CHAPTER ONE

The two men waiting on the platform looked bored. The one who seemed to be the station master wore a shiny black suit. A cigarette dangled from his lips. The other, a fat man in blue overalls, was waving a dim lantern in the direction of the train driver. I picked up my case and started down the aisle. The compartment was almost empty; the other few passengers were sprawled out asleep. I jumped down onto the platform and looked around.

A man about six foot nine, 250 pounds, clambered down from the first class coach. He stood there gazing about as if expecting someone to come up and thrust a bunch of flowers in his hand. The fat man blew a whistle and shouted an insult at the driver. His companion came over to me and smiled a greeting.

"You must be Morales," he said, without removing his cigarette.

I smiled back. "No, Galvan's the name."

"Andres Galvan!" He held out his hand. "I'm Carranza. The station master. Which boardinghouse are you in?"

I was about to ask him which one he recommended when I saw the soldiers. The taller of the two had his rifle trained half-heartedly on me; the other, a blackhaired youngster with his helmet pulled down over his ears, lurked in the background, almost out of sight. The sergeant with them had one of those moustaches they cultivate just to scare conscripts.

"Your papers," he barked.

The station master put on his most huskily persuasive voice. "This is Galvan, the singer. He's OK."

I handed over my ID card. The sergeant examined it, turning it in all directions, then wrote down the details in his notebook.

"You here for the celebrations?" he asked without looking at me.

"Yes. Mr Suarez booked me."

"Captain Suarez," he corrected me.

"Captain Suarez," I agreed.

He handed back my papers. Then, glancing over my shoulder, he cried out: "Halt!"

The huge figure that had stepped out of the first class compartment was about to disappear through the waiting room door. The two soldiers levelled their rifles at him. They didn't have to be crack shots to keep him covered; his back was as broad as a dining table.

He dropped his bag on the floor and turned to

8

look at them without betraying any surprise. He had a sad look on his face, as though weary of dragging his enormous bulk through the world. He was wearing a long leather jacket and a pair of jeans that had seen better days.

"Up against the wall," the sergeant shouted, pointing at a poster for a local restaurant. The big fellow didn't wait to be asked: he put his hands in the air, and leaned against the poster, legs spread wide. The dark-haired soldier searched him for a few seconds, then gave up. The sergeant examined the man's ID card under the yellow station light a few feet away.

"Rocha..." the station master said from somewhere behind my back.

The train pulled out, drowning the rest of what he was saying.

"What was that?"

"Rocha," he repeated, pointing to the giant who watched without moving a muscle as the soldiers went through his things. "Got a good punch. A bit slow for my liking though."

I studied the man. He didn't look exactly speedy. Or very alert, though with people that size you never can tell.

"I wouldn't know," I said. "Never saw him."

"I did, on TV," the station. master continued. "When he knocked out that Paraguayan guy. He's got a lethal punch, but he's too slow." He bent over to whisper: "Is it true he's finished?"

9

"Why should he be finished?"

"That's what they say. You're from Buenos Aires, you ought to know."

I told him again I didn't know Rocha, and walked out through the deserted waiting room. An avenue lined with trees in blossom seemed to lead to the town centre. I walked slowly down it. On the corner was a waste lot overrun with weeds. In the middle of it someone had built a kind of hut using two thick branches for support. A couple of blocks further on I passed a bar where half a dozen men were playing cards and drinking. I looked in at them, but kept on going, and crossed the street. A warm, gentle breeze was stirring the leaves of the acacias. An army jeep went by, with the soldiers who had checked us out in the station. I remembered that before leaving Buenos Aires I'd made myself a ham and cheese sandwich. I put my case down on a car and took out the plastic bag. I walked on, chewing at the rubbery bread, trying to imagine from the old, grey housefronts what the people in a town like this could be up to at ten o'clock at night. Suddenly I heard thunderous footsteps behind me, as though King Kong had broken loose again. Peering round, I saw Rocha hurrying along the middle of the street. He flapped along as if intent on squashing every ant in his path. I stood and waited for him. It was obvious he wasn't built for dodging and weaving in the ring. He plunged along head down, his bag slung over his back. He stopped in front of me, out of breath.

"I finally caught up with you," he boomed.

His eyes seemed small for such an enormous face; his nose was the typical veteran's pancake. I stared at him, not knowing what to say. Finally I came out with: "Everything OK?"

He smiled, and dropped his bag. "Fine," he said, looking at me with a strange coyness. "I've got one of your records. The one with *One for The Road* on it."

He said it as if he were the only person in the whole country who had a record of mine. I swallowed the last bit of my sandwich, waiting for him to go on.

"You here to sing?" he asked, wiping his neck with a handkerchief.

"Tomorrow, for the town anniversary celebrations."

As soon as I said this, he grinned contentedly, nodding his head. "So you came for the dough too, did you?"

I thought that was a bit much, considering he was the proud owner of one of my records. I shrugged as if to say, "That's the way it goes." Again he nodded.

"Rocha's the name; good to meet you." He held out an arm as long and thick as a fireman's hose.

"Glad to meet you," I said. He picked up his bag and gathered himself together until every part

11

of his body was ready to move off again. As we walked along, he kept staring at me. When we reached the corner, he gave me a hearty slap on the back and roared: "You've got a great voice, dammit."

CHAPTER TWO

The landlady showed us a room at the back. It gave onto a good-sized patio full of flowers, around which ran an open verandah. A cat asleep on one of the beds scarcely bothered to open its eyes to see who was coming in. Rocha stared at the walls, the ceiling, the crucifixes over the beds.

"I don't like it," he said. "No windows."

The landlady was taken aback, and retreated to the doorway, waiting for us to make up our minds.

"Haven't you got one at the front?" he asked, discouraged. "I need a window, air, plenty of fresh air. I'm a boxer, see."

Nobody would ever have imagined he was a priest or a businessman.

"And my friend here sings," he added. "We both live by our lungs."

"I can make you up a room at the front, but it'll cost you more."

Rocha nodded. "Good idea, granma, good idea," he said, brightening.

"That'll be a hundred extra because I have to prepare it specially."

It was more than I wanted to pay, but Rocha got in first.

"Don't worry about the money, granma. Give us the key so we can go get something to eat. Is it too late to find somewhere open in this hole?"

The landlady wasn't too keen on the crack about "this hole", but told us where there was a restaurant.

I would have made do with my sandwich, but Rocha's enthusiasm was catching, so I decided to go with him.

It was the kind of restaurant where people go to show off their new outfits. Rocha went in and stood looking around. Any stranger would have aroused interest, but a giant like him was a special treat. By the time we were halfway across the room everybody was staring at us. Rocha kept smiling and nodding, though nobody returned his greeting. Half a dozen tables were occupied; most of the diners were on their last course. I hurried to the far side to be out of the way, but just as I was sitting at the corner table I heard a call from across the room.

"Here, Galvan, this is the best place."

He wasn't shouting, but he wasn't exactly whispering a racing tip either. He was at a table in the centre of the room, plainly surprised the waiter hadn't yet come to take his order. I walked back as unobtrusively as I could and sat opposite him.

"What are you hiding for? Can't you see we're

celebrities here?"

His eyes shone warmly. The waiter came up and said, "Good evening, gentlemen," but this was aimed exclusively at me. His fair hair was scraped forward from the back of his head in a useless effort to hide an embarrassing bald patch. I ordered a steak and fries. Rocha wanted a complete barbecue for two and a litre of wine, but the waiter looked to me for confirmation.

"In that case, you won't want the steak," he said.

"Yes, for me," I told him.

"And a barbecue for two," Rocha insisted.

"There's a lot of meat in our barbecues," the waiter said, again addressing me.

Rocha took him by the arm, and pushed him on his way.

"Barbecue for two," he said firmly.

Baldy walked away without another word.

"It's not a good idea to upset waiters," Rocha scolded himself. "They can ruin your food before they serve you. I know, I was a waiter once."

"Not out here in the country," I said brightly. "People aren't so spiteful."

He guffawed. The sound made me nervous. "Don't get out of Buenos Aires much, do you?" he said eventually, running his left hand through his thick, greasy hair. It was then I caught sight of the scar right across the back.

Two men at the next table were watching us as they chatted quietly. One, a young fellow in a grey suit, had a vaguely unsavoury look; the other, a short man about fifty, wore an immense red bow tie and a white shirt. His black suit was impeccable, but the vest was too tight.

The waiter brought our food and wine. Rocha bent over the plates to examine them. "Go ahead," he said, "they haven't spat in it."

In spite of everything, I did eat. Before I'd finished the fries, Rocha had polished off all the barbecue and the bottle of wine. Then he called to the waiter as if hailing a taxi. This time the man kept a safe distance.

"Strawberries for two, and coffee," he ordered.

I sat there fuming at him while he devoured the last piece of bread. "I came here to work, not to stuff myself silly," I said. "Who do you think you are, Mohammed Ali?"

He stared at me as if he didn't get what I meant. "Did you ever see Mohammed Ali?" he muttered.

"A couple of times, on TV," I said.

He sat in silence; a look of false modesty spread across his face. "I sparred with him at the Argentine Boxing Federation the first time he came down here."

He leaned back to see what effect the news would have on me.

"So?"

"So it's not everyone who can say they sparred with Ali."

Rocha didn't even notice the waiter had brought our strawberries and coffee. He pushed his seat back and put up his fists.

"I soon worked him out. Everybody else gave him room; they let him lead with his left and dance around. They were asking for a hiding."

"This is no place for a show," I warned him.

He wasn't listening. He threw a right cross, stopping the punch inches from my face. I glanced around surreptitiously. A young couple was leaving; the man was helping his girlfriend with her coat. The little fellow with the red bow tie was on his own now and seemed to want to join us.

"That's how he sent all those meatballs to the deck, see? But I closed him down, and then what could he do?"

He dropped his fists, waiting for my reply.

"Your strawberries," I said, pointing.

He seemed surprised to find the bowl in front of him. He finished them off in less than a minute.

"I'll order another bottle, if you'll share it," he suggested.

I was worried the wine might make him worse.

"Let's try somewhere else. They're going to close here."

I looked around the room. The only other person left was our diminutive neighbour, who

17

couldn't take his eyes off us. His hair was slicked back neatly, with a high parting. He was so tiny only his head and shoulders showed above the table cloth.

"OK," Rocha sighed, and called the waiter over again. He came scurrying up, relieved we were leaving. Rocha took out a battered leather wallet.

"This is on me," he said loftily. There was no way I was going to be in his debt, so I said: "No, no, let's go halves."

He smiled. A smile to emphasise my petty-mindedness and his own false sense of dignity. He pulled out some banknotes and proffered them to the waiter. Now it was the waiter's turn to smile as he stood facing Rocha.

"That's already been taken care of," he said, glancing over at our neighbour, who by now was on his feet. "This gentleman is paying for your meal," he explained, in a voice that oozed respect for our benefactor.

I was about to thank the man when Rocha blurted out, like a whiny kid who's had his lollipop taken from him: "What gentleman?"

"Exequiel Aguila Bayo, at your service," the little man said. He'd already slid across to our table, and was holding out a plump and sweaty hand. After the presentation, he waved a carved wooden cane in the direction of the door.

"Will you have a drink with me, gentlemen?" he said, smiling, the bow tie bobbing on his chubby neck as he spoke. "I'd welcome a chance to talk to you."

CHAPTER THREE

We crossed the square. It was a warm night and spring had filled the flowerbeds. Aguila Bayo cut a red carnation and delicately placed it in his lapel. None of us spoke: he leaned elegantly on his cane as he walked, and Rocha was trying hard not to go too fast for him. I fell behind, pausing to breathe in the night air and look at the dim lights of the square. All at once, Aguila Bayo stopped, raised his head, threw open his arms as if to embrace the whole universe, and exclaimed: "Gentlemen, though you may not think it, this town has seen great suffering."

Rocha slowed, and with some difficulty turned to look down at our host. I stopped as well, so Aguila Bayo was left standing, a bit idiotic, between the two of us, his arms outstretched, pointing up at the church tower with his cane. He sighed, let his arms drop, and went on in a low voice.

"We really need something to celebrate," he said. Then, pointing at me: "You will be singing in the Avenue Theatre before a select audience. Members of the armed forces will be present, and,

20

if you promise not to sing anything too racy, so will the three representatives of the Church. It may be a trifle boring for you, but that's what you're being paid for, isn't it? And that's the main thing."

He turned to Rocha. "Your appeal is more popular, of course. You'll be in the Union and Progress Club. You'll have to watch out, Sepulveda has a lightning right. Seven knockouts in a row."

Rocha spat against a tree.

"If he beats you, he'll be a contender."

Rocha spat again, but said nothing. I was wondering about my audience. "You mean my concert isn't open to everyone?"

"Of course not." The tone of his voice was meant to show how highly the authorities thought of me.

"What about that drink?" Rocha butted in. He was leaning against the same tree he had just spat on. Aguila Bayo looked at him and gave a forced laugh.

"We're nearly there. I've got some bottles of Burgundy at home. Or whisky, if you'd rather."

There were two taxis outside the Avenue Theatre and two helmeted soldiers carrying submachine guns, like the pair we had met at the station. Our companion greeted them; the driver in the first taxi responded with a "how are you, sir?" One of the soldiers raised his free hand to his helmet and saluted respectfully.

We walked on ten blocks. Aguila Bayo lived in a large old mansion, its facade freshly painted. Beside the front door a brass plate announced: "Exequiel Aguila Bayo, Attorney-at-Law." There was a window each side of the door, and at one corner an iron gate, which presumably led to the back of the house. Aguila Bayo opened the front door and ushered us in. The sound of the Beegees drifted from some distant room. We were shown into the study, a large room with a long glass-fronted bookcase that contained a bound collection of *The Law Journal* up to 1967. There was a heap of files on the desk, around which three leather armchairs stood collecting dust. A painting of General San Martin victorious at the battle of Chacabuco hung on the far wall. To the right of it was a photograph of a gloomy fellow with an old-fashioned hair style. Seeing me examining it, our lawyer friend commented: "Ortiz, the only brave and decent civilian president Argentina's ever had."

Rocha grunted in agreement. Aguila Bayo waved us to sit in the armchairs, and positioned himself behind his desk. I sat down as carefully as I could to avoid getting dirty, but the big fellow brazenly took out his handkerchief and began to dust his chair. I lit a cigarette; when Aguila Bayo saw me, he emptied an ashtray into the wastepaper basket and brought it to me, just as I stood up to go and fetch it. We met halfway; he laid a friendly hand on my arm and asked, almost whispering in my ear: "What can I offer you? Whisky? A decent wine? Some coffee?"

Then he spoke to Rocha. "I expect you'd like a glass of Burgundy?"

Rocha had engulfed the armchair and seemed settled in. "So long as it's not white," he said.

Aguila Bayo gave a little chuckle which ended in a reproof: "Burgundy is never white, my friend, that's why it's called Burgundy. You'll see."

He went out into the corridor. We sat in silence for a while until Rocha whistled to me. We were only a couple of yards from each other, but he obviously had a mania for whistling. I looked at him.

"Nice man, eh?" he said.

I raised a finger to my lips for him not to say any more. He nodded. We sat staring at each other in silence until the lawyer re-appeared.

"Friends," he said, again all but disappearing behind his desk, "I asked you here to share a drink not simply because I like what I've seen of you, but also, I must admit, out of a sense of professional duty."

Now he was getting to the point. He paused theatrically and seemed to grow visibly in size. "You know as well as I do that it is no easy matter these days to carry through a proper celebration. Making sure, in these difficult times for our nation, that the event isn't spoiled is no piece of cake, if you'll pardon the expression."

"No, of course not," Rocha said.

"You're quite right there," the lawyer said, taking him into his confidence. "Why, these days it even takes courage to sing the national anthem at school."

He contemplated us for a while. I put out my cigarette, watching him closely.

"Courage, discipline, and patriotism," he pronounced, spreading his hands on the desk. "Hence the need for someone to organise and plan - which is where I, in all modesty, come in."

Rocha nodded again, frowning. "So you're the one who'll get me a dressing gown, are you?"

The lawyer was flustered. "Doesn't a boxer of your..." he hesitated "...of your calibre...have his own dressing gown?"

It seemed to me Rocha was blushing.

"I left it behind," he said, staring at the floor as though to avoid Exequiel Aguila Bayo's reproachful eyes.

Our organising genius was about to say something, but at that moment the door opened and a young woman came in.

She was wearing a high-necked flowery summer dress that was slightly too long. She was tall, slim, and had a pleasant face free of make-up. Her long black hair was held up with a comb. She must have been about twenty, and didn't look the type to be the heart-breaker of Colonia Vela. She peered around timidly and cautiously, as if her eyes would see only what they were allowed to. As she left the tray on the desk top, she smiled sweetly at us.

"My daughter," Aguila Bayo explained. "My little Martha."

Both of us stood up to shake her dainty white hand. As I did so, I heard her father say one of those phrases you never hear any more: "She's the light of my life."

His words hung in the air. I sat down again and looked at the others: the lawyer was standing behind his desk, the palms of his hands flat on the files, gazing proudly at his daughter; Rocha's tiny brown eyes were roving from the girl's smooth throat to her unpromising neckline down to her thin, pale arms. Gently, she withdrew her hand from his huge paws and turned to serve us. When she'd finished, she excused herself and left as quietly as she had entered. Rocha slowly lowered himself back into his chair, his eyes still fixed on the door Martha had closed behind her.

"This is a real Burgundy," our lawyer friend said, rolling the wine on his palate for a few seconds. This seemed to wake Rocha up. He raised the glass to his lips and downed the wine in one.

"Good stuff," he said, staring at his empty glass.

Dismayed, Aguila Bayo fell back into his chair. "What kind of dressing gown do you need?"

"What's that?" Rocha's mind was elsewhere.

Our lawyer friend picked up a pencil and

opened his notebook. "I can see you're tired, so I won't bother you any more this evening. I was asking what sort of dressing gown you need."

"Oh, anything, so long as it's my size."

I tried to imagine where on earth Aguila Bayo could find a dressing gown big enough. If there was a spare circus tent handy, perhaps. He wrote something down in his book, then looked at me.

"You have all you need, I trust. Tomorrow you can meet the band and rehearse with them. The *bandoneon* player isn't bad."

I nodded, finished my coffee and looked suitably worn out.

"One last thing, boys. If I were you, I'd try to avoid all contact with the public until the day you perform. Also, if you talk to the press here I'd like to ask as a personal favour that you particularly stress the effort and dedication the armed forces have put into organising this celebration for the town."

He noted something else in his book, then suddenly stood up. "Until tomorrow at Mass then."

Before we could reply he went over to the door, opened it, and called softly: "Martha! our guests are leaving!"

Rocha and I exchanged glances. Martha glided silently into the room. She had removed the comb, and her hair hung in waves over her shoulders. She was holding a miserable four-page broadsheet, full of ads and almost illegible type. She opened it and showed Rocha.

"Look, your photo is in the paper," she said in a voice strained with shyness.

It was Rocha, but ten years younger; his features were hard to distinguish in the blurred inky columns. The headline read: "Hard-hitting Tony Rocha Arrives Today in Colonia Vela".

"It's the photo they used in the Buenos Aires newspapers," Rocha said, proud of himself, "the day I beat Murillo at Luna Park."

I said goodnight to Martha and stepped out onto the sidewalk with her father. I realised I had a headache; the night seemed to be getting hotter. Rocha whispered something quickly to Martha as they said goodbye in the hall. Aguila Bayo shook hands with us yet again, and smiled broadly. I was in a hurry to get to bed. At the street corner, Rocha patted me on the back and said, "We'll be there for Mass, won't we, eh?"

I kept my mouth shut. I was beginning to wish I'd asked for a room of my own. He went on, "What's with you? Don't you believe in God or something?"

I walked on without replying. He grabbed my arm, but spoke less gruffly. "Do it for me, Galvan. I always say a prayer before a fight."

"I've got a headache," I told him. I crossed the street and speeded up. He was back alongside me in an instant.

"Why didn't you say so? When we get to our room I'll give you a face massage - you'll see, I'm an expert. I haven't got a trainer, see, so if I get a headache before a fight...I have to know about these things, don't I?"

I pulled up short. "Get off my back, will you? You can go to Mass or throw yourself in the lake for all I care, but leave me alone! I don't want to hear another word from you tonight!"

This time he didn't follow me. As soon as I got in, I switched off the light.

28

CHAPTER FOUR

Someone was shaking me like the house was on fire. I woke with a start and saw Rocha's huge hand clutching my shoulder. He'd put all the lights on and was standing at my bedside, swaying on his feet. It took me a few seconds to wake up and realise my head was still aching. Before I could shout for him to get out of my sight, he grinned and said, "I've brought you an admirer."

Standing in the doorway was a small man wearing a suit with drainpipe trousers and a hat like Carlos Gardel. He was leaning on his guitar, as though posing for a photograph.

"Forgive me," I said, "I'm not feeling well and I'd like to go back to sleep, if it's not too much to ask."

Rocha looked disappointed. "This kid knows how to handle a guitar," he said, jerking a thumb in his direction. "Come on in Romero! Come and say hello to the maestro!" he bawled.

Romero almost fell on top of me he was so keen to shake my hand.

"A great kid," Rocha repeated, starting to

undress. The kid must have had at least sixty years under his belt.

"Delighted to meet you, senor Galvan," he said, returning to his start position draped over the guitar.

"My pleasure," I replied. "A real pleasure meeting you. How about us getting together for a coffee and a chat tomorrow? The thing is, I'm a bit tired right now."

"The intensity you create in *Honeysuckle* goes far beyond any intrinsic merit of the melody itself," he went on, unruffled.

"Thanks," I said. "We can talk about it tomorrow."

"Listening to you is like reaching out and touching the honeysuckle with one's ears."

I realised I wasn't going to get rid of him that easily.

I reached for my pack of cigarettes, but before I got there Romero was offering me one of his.

"But those new tangos you've been singing, those...what'd you call them...those protest tangos, are beyond me, to be honest."

He gave me a light.

"Beyond me too," I replied. "I haven't sung them for ages."

He gestured with his free hand to show he understood, and leaned forward confidentially.

"This is no time for taking risks," he said. He

looked around for somewhere to sit, but was in two minds about it. "Anyway," he went on, adopting a critical tone, "tangos and politics don't mix."

When I didn't reply, he puffed on his cigarette and added, "That's how I see it, anyway."

"So you sing as well, do you?" I said, for want of anything better to say.

He grinned modestly down at his guitar, and stroked it like a pet dog. "I've done a bit," he said. "I've had artistic leanings since I was a boy."

I was in for his life story. In the other bed, Rocha began to snore like an elephant, but Romero was oblivious to him. "And I was fortunate enough to meet Carlos Gardel."

Not another one, I thought. His voice turned solemn. "It was in Tandil, back in '33. I was only a kid then, of course."

"And Carlos told you your future lay in your throat."

"Exactly." his eyes narrowed. "He took me back to his dressing room and asked me to sing for him. I gave him *Lucky Charm*. I remember I had a cheap little guitar, a Parkington..."

I was thinking Gardel must have been a man of boundless patience.

"Later I tried my luck several times in Buenos Aires but never got anywhere."

He lowered his gaze again, as if the pain of recollection was too much for him. All at once, he lifted one foot onto my bed, swivelled his guitar down into position on his chest beneath his bootlace tie and strummed the chords of a tune that was meant to be *She Came Back One Night*. He paused.

"Someone famous today, and who I won't name, shafted me just as I was about to start with D'Agostino's orchestra." He paused again. "Back in '48."

I nodded, so he'd get on with it. He started with *Malena*, but broke off again. "In those days to get anywhere you had to be Peronist..."

He scrutinised me. When I didn't move a muscle, he went on, "It's not that I was against him, far from it..." he plucked a low note.

"And nowadays?"

"Well, nowadays...sometimes I get the feeling it's too late for me. Though there's still hope, especially when a singer of your reputation has the chance to listen to me."

"I meant, do you think things are any different nowadays?"

"Well, look," he decided to confide in me, "politics has always brought me bad luck - that's why I said before that tangos and politics don't mix. Take this town: back in '74 we'd got together our tango orchestra with some money from the town hall, from Don Ignacio Fuentes, who was the mayor then - may he rest in peace - when all hell broke loose and nearly the whole place was

32

burned down."

"What hell?"

"Here, in Colonia Vela," and he added, sounding proud of it, "twenty-two people killed in one day. It was no joke, I can tell you. Luckily the military have been here three years now. They've built a school and a barracks."

Rocha turned in his bed, snorted, and the rhythm of his snores changed. I put my cigarette out and turned to pat my pillow. When our guest didn't take the hint and carried on standing there, I yawned and stared at him.

"I'm grateful for your kind attention," he said, strumming his guitar again. "I'd like to dedicate this next song to you - it was composed by myself and Don Juan Honorio - and has not yet been performed in public. It goes without saying that if you like it you can feel free to include it in your repertory. It's called *Sadness of Forgetting*.

Before I could open my mouth to protest, he launched into it. He had a weak reedy voice, and a drunk singing the national anthem would have hit more notes. Somewhere in the middle he began a frightful caterwauling. Rocha shot bolt upright in alarm, and sat there still three-quarters asleep.

"What's going on?" he asked, his tiny eyes opening wide. Romero ploughed on with the song, like a performer ignoring a restless audience. He struck the chords and was about to give it all he had when Rocha got out of bed, took him by his jacket, lifted him three feet off the floor and carried him across to the door.

"Go shout on the football pitch, you bum," he grunted. Undeterred, Romero was still plucking at his guitar with his legs running in mid-air. I watched them leave, heard the sound of the guitar and Romero's voice for a few seconds more, then a crash as something hit the ground.

Rocha came back in and headed straight for bed, still half-asleep. Before clambering in he shouted furiously, "Are you crazy? What d'you mean bringing someone in here to sing at this time of night?"

CHAPTER FIVE

At 7.30 the next morning we were wakened by a soldier sent by Aguila Bayo. He said Mass was at nine and stood in the doorway to wait. I lifted a blind and looked into the street; a black limousine stood outside. Even its tires looked polished. A tiny Argentine pennant fluttered from the radio aerial, and the national coat of arms adorned the license plate.

In five minutes Rocha washed and dressed. I told the soldier I preferred to walk, which meant he had to telephone to ask permission not to take me with him. He and Rocha left. I watched through the window as Rocha got into the back seat and the soldier closed the door for him before getting in behind the wheel. Three old women and a couple of pensioners applauded as the limousine moved off. I finished dressing and went out into the street.

It was a flat town with wide streets like one of many in Buenos Aires province. The tallest building had three storeys and was a kind of shopping arcade facing the square. Families were out for a stroll, and the loudspeakers were playing garbled pop music which all of a sudden was interrupted by the announcement, possibly, that Mass was about to start. The passers-by began to disappear, as though the church bells meant some kind of morning curfew.

There was a bar on the corner. I ordered a coffee with croissants, but since this was a public holiday, had to make do with toast. I don't know whether the waiter recognised me, but before bringing my order he whispered something into the bar owner's ear. A photo of Gardel with Leguisamo hung over the counter. I sat staring at Gardel until a friendly voice made me turn around.

"Will you buy me a coffee, sir?"

He was wrapped in a light grey raincoat that had more black blotches than a stormy sky.

"Of course," I said. "Order yourself one. Why don't you sit down?"

He looked astonished. He glanced over at the bar owner and asked, "Are you sure?"

"Didn't you want a coffee?"

"And I can sit with you?"

I nodded. He sat down gingerly, as if afraid the seat would give way. He pulled an old, clean thermos out of his raincoat pocket and set it on the table in front of him. He sat following his own movements while I ordered his coffee and more toast. He watched himself stretch out his legs under the table as though they had a life of their own. Then he noticed the mirror to his right and began to watch the whole reflected scene: him and me. I offered him a cigarette: he looked at it, reached out his hand, rubbing his fingers to get rid of any dirt that might prevent his enjoying the feel, and finally took it.

"I know you," he said.

He unbuttoned his coat with a naturally delicate gesture that hinted at a long-lost elegance. The waiter brought his order and gave him a hard look before he went away.

"Of course I know you. From hearing you, I mean." He looked at himself again in the mirror. It's ages since I sat here...It was me who made this bar, you know."

"What d'you mean?"

There must have been a note of disbelief or condescension in my voice, because he suddenly threw me a cold, steely look. He chewed on his beard with yellow stained teeth. "I used to be a bricklayer."

I sipped my coffee without a word.

"At the start, this was a high class place." He paused. "That was years ago."

I took a bite of my toast. The street outside was still deserted, and we were the only people in the bar apart from a youngster chatting to the waiter.

"Later it got less fashionable, and they allowed everyone in. Everyone except me that is. I come here to bum a coffee - I put it in my thermos and clear off before the owner gets mad. There's nearly always someone willing to buy the town idiot a coffee."

A fly circled the table then flew off, banging against the window that gave on to the square.

"Who says you're an idiot?"

"The people here."

"And are you or aren't you?"

"What does it matter? At the moment it's you the bar owner thinks is an idiot for letting me sit here. If you went off to the toilet, he'd kick me out."

We got on with our breakfasts in silence, as our cigarettes burnt down in the ashtray. "You came for the celebration," he said finally.

I said I had.

"Never been in Colonia Vela before?"

"No."

"Then you won't know what good times we used to have in the old days, when nobody came along to tell you when you had to be happy. They went on as long as we felt like it, or until we were exhausted."

"When was that?"

"Oh, a long while ago; when I was a young man just arrived from the South."

"What happened afterwards?"

He chuckled, brushed the fly away, and motioned for me to give him another cigarette.

"Afterwards times changed, and I grew old. We all grew old. You can see there are hardly any young people left in the town."

"How come?"

He gazed at me as though trying to figure out if I really was stupid or was putting it on. In the end he shrugged and blew out cigarette smoke. "A lot were killed, others simply left."

I asked him if he'd like a brandy and he said he'd be delighted. I ordered them. The church bells rang out a second time, and people began to leave Mass. The square was soon full of life again. It was impossible to imagine where so many people had come from unless the church could pack in a thousand worshippers. The bar started to fill up. Without exception, every newcomer stared in our direction. It was comical to see out of the corner of my eye the way they were all whispering about us.

"I feel sorry for them," he said suddenly. "They sell their soul for next to nothing, then they go to Mass to ask for forgiveness."

"Not everyone is like that."

"No, of course not. I'm not that stupid. But these people, the Sunday morning crowd...take a good look at them. Nearly all of them have a dead relative. Their youngest relation, the idiot of the family. They console each other as though it was an epidemic that killed them."

"And what did you do when the epidemic was

around?"

"Me? The same as them. See, hear, and keep my mouth shut. The older you get, the more you cling on to things, the more you accept, the more scared you are of losing whatever trash it is you've heaped together."

He gazed disdainfully around the bar, then down at the ashtray.

"Why are you telling me all this?" I asked.

"No idea. The need to talk, I guess. I used to have a friend I'd spend all night talking to. He was a real philosopher. He used to say that having a bit of money gets you nowhere and is boring, so it's better to have nothing at all."

"Who was this philosopher?"

"A bum like me. I couldn't tell you he was someone who had this or that so you could place him. But he was sharp all right. He knew about life."

"What became of him?"

"They killed him. I had trouble getting his remains into a bag to bury him."

"Why did they do that?"

"They mistook him for someone trying to escape one night. That was when the military had just arrived and were blasting heads off right, left and centre."

At that moment Martha entered hesitantly at the corner door, as if surprised at appearing in front of so many people. She must have been

40

overwhelmed by all the stares, because she turned back to grab her father's arm as he came in, saying hello to everyone. Rocha was behind them, followed by two men a head shorter than he. Rocha stood looking from table to table until, finally, he saw me and came over.

"Where'd you get to?" he growled, like some cheap gangster.

"What's that to you?" I replied.

"We were expecting you at Mass. Aguila Bayo is furious. You showed him up in front of everyone."

It was only then that he noticed who I was with. He stared at him dumbfounded, then jerked his head at him. "Where'd you dig up this hobo?"

My new-found friend looked at himself again in the mirror and smiled. "This gentleman offered me breakfast," he said.

Rocha stared at him. When he spoke to me, the doubt in his voice showed he was tempted to believe him: "What are you up to now? Last night you bring someone back for a party in our room; now you're having breakfast with a tramp. Are you nuts?"

"Come and sit down. What'll you have?"

He bent down to whisper in my ear, with a gesture of such exaggerated secrecy it could have been seen as far as the station. "Our lawyer friend is angry with you," he said.

"Because I didn't go to Mass?"

He nodded solemnly. "Athletes and artistes were supposed to be at church."

The tramp looked at us with a gleam in his eye. Rocha bent down again, and knocked over a cup with his elbow. "Come on," he said, winking at me, "I'll help you make it up with him."

"Nothing doing," I said. "I came here to work, not to go to confession."

He couldn't seem to take it in. He glanced around anxiously at Aguila Bayo, who was chatting with friends at his table. The tramp finished wiping off the coffee Rocha had spilled on him, looked out the window and said, "I'll be on my way."

He stood up, slowly buttoned his coat, and held out his hand to me. "Thanks for breakfast," he said.

I stood up and shook hands. Halfway to the door he halted and turned to look at the other customers. His long hair, unkempt beard and discoloured moustache hid his face, but his eyes gleamed so brightly his gaze parted the smoke-filled bar. He said something I couldn't make out above all the noise and then left. Rocha took hold of my arm and again brought his snout down to my ear level to bawl, "Come out to the toilet, I have to talk to you."

"Tell me here. I don't want anything to do with you."

He lowered himself reluctantly into the chair the tramp had vacated. "Our lawyer friend's in a fury with you."

"You already said that. What's he so upset about?"

"You seen the slogan?"

"What slogan?"

"In the street. Opposite the church. 'Andres Galvan sings for murderers' it says."

"What?" I started in my seat. I could tell he was not joking.

"That's what it said. The soldiers are busy whitewashing it out."

He gazed at me in commiseration. He stretched out an enormous arm and shook my shoulder to console me. "You been in trouble, friend?"

I told him I hadn't. He squeezed my shoulder blade all the more and in his huskiest voice assured me, "You can count on me."

Much to the other customers' delight, he went on kneading my shoulder.

"So that's why Aguila Bayo's furious, is it?" I asked.

He dropped his arm. "He got mad when you didn't show up at Mass."

"After he saw the slogan."

"Yes, but that's not your fault, Galvan. It must have been someone trying to set the cops on you."

"You don't understand, do you? How long is it since you've read the papers?"

"What's that got to do with it? I read the paper

43

yesterday - and my photo was in it and yours wasn't, that's why..."

"Do you have to be so dumb?" I said, realising I was shouting. Rocha didn't budge; he stared at me with his watery eyes and flushed face.

"Don't say that," he protested. "Never in front of other people."

"Let's carry on outside," I said in the same cold tone.

His eyes glinted ominously. "First, take back what you just said."

I became aware of the silence around us. A silence which made us the centre of attraction and which didn't seem to trouble Rocha in the least. "All right," I said, "I take it back."

He relaxed and heaved a sigh of relief now he wouldn't have to beat the daylights out of me. He was about to ask for a cigarette when he remembered he was still annoyed with me, so he played with a spoon instead. "I have to get back to Aguila Bayo," he said.

"Show me the slogan first."

He hesitated, glancing over at Aguila Bayo's table, then stood up. I steered him over towards the door, and he let himself be led.

We crossed the square. It was nearly noon, and there were fewer people about. A green Ford Falcon was parked outside the theatre. A fat man in shirtsleeves was standing by it, sweating profusely, his machine gun lying across the front.

44

Further down, an army jeep was parked by the wall of the Spanish Club. Two soldiers were working with brushes and buckets, while a third sat at the wheel of the jeep. About a dozen people looked on from the square.

"There," Rocha said. "That's where it was written."

The soldiers had whitewashed the wall, but still visible were the words:

ANDRES GALVAN
SINGS FOR MURDERERS

"Wait till they've gone," I said.

The jeep screeched off, and as it turned the corner we crossed the street. From close up, it was easier to see the slogan. It had been painted with black aerosol, and would have needed five coats of whitewash to obliterate it completely. I found what I was looking for up in the corner. I took Rocha by the arm and dragged him over to it. He didn't say a thing, but moved his head nearer and then back from the freshly painted wall to convince himself it wasn't an illusion.

IN EVERY ROCHA
A TORTURER

He read it five or six times, barely moving his lips, stressing his name. Then he turned around to gaze at me dejectedly. "I never hurt anybody," he said. "I've never quarrelled with a soul, so why did they write that?"

He went over to the square and sat on a bench.

He seemed crushed, as though he'd just heard terrible news.

The church bell struck twelve, and all of a sudden the square had emptied. The sun was making me sweat, and I needed a drink. I was about to say so to Rocha when the Falcon parked outside the theatre glided slowly over to us. The fat guy with the machine gun got out; behind him came a dark-haired character of around twenty-five perched on high-heeled boots. He was wearing denim jeans and jacket, with dark sunglasses. A revolver butt stuck out of his belt. He must have taken himself for Gary Cooper. The fat man slung his machine gun over his shoulder to show this was a social call. "Andres Galvan, tango's golden voice," he said.

I stared at him. He turned and said to Gary Cooper: "Goyeneche, Rivero, and Galvan; forget the rest." He paused: "Except for Gardel of course."

The dark-haired kid didn't reply. He looked more like a Rolling Stones fan. Fatso turned to Rocha. "You're no Monzon," he cackled, "still, I wouldn't like to try out your uppercut."

Rocha stared at the machine gun. He was still upset. The fat man spoke to his companion again. "You like boxing, don't you? Why not get his autograph?"

The kid clumped off back to the car and returned with a notebook. He sauntered along, taking his time to reach Rocha. He held out the open notebook. Fatso got out a pen and Rocha signed his name, then handed the book back. The fat man passed it to me.

"I don't give autographs," I said.

The fat man contemplated me for a while, then laughed. "You're kidding," he said. "Rivero signed for me. With a dedication too."

"Rivero signs autographs. It's not my style."

He lowered the machine gun from his shoulder to the ground. He was covered in sweat and didn't seem in the mood for an argument.

"When I catch whoever painted those slogans I'll bring him to you on a plate," he said. He held out the book but I wouldn't take it.

The atmosphere was becoming tense.

"Go on, sign it, don't be mean," he said.

"Don't get me wrong, but I never sign autographs," I explained.

He stood there in silence, then went over and sat next to Rocha. He was tapping his knee with the open notebook, where half a page was filled with Rocha's writing.

" 'Sings for murderers', " he said. "They really had it in for you, didn't they?" He laughed a hollow laugh. He took out a handkerchief and wiped his forehead. Suddenly he stopped laughing and shouted at me like a sergeant major.

"I break my ass so that you can have a nice quiet time! For a week now I've been having two

47

hours sleep and eating nothing but sandwiches so those creeps can have their celebration, and you, you won't sign me an autograph!"

"Listen," I started to protest, "it's a rule I have..."

He bellowed so loud he must have been heard for ten blocks around: "Stick it up your ass! You hear me? Up your ass!"

Rocha looked at us, waiting for me to react. Perhaps he was expecting me to take my coat off and challenge the guy to a fight. I heard myself say something grotesque: "Take that back."

That's what you get from being around people like Rocha. Fatso stood up and glanced over at his friend as though to confirm what he had heard.

"What did you say?" he asked, plodding over towards me. I was relieved to see he was dragging the machine gun along and didn't seem inclined to use it. I decided it would be wiser to apologise, but Rocha called out in a challenging voice: "He asked you to take back what you said!"

The fat man allowed this to sink in, then smiled faintly. "Buddies, are we?" he said wearily. "Think that because you're in the newspapers you can treat the police like shit, don't you?"

The other one came up and said, running his fingers through his black hair: "Not here, chief. We'd better take them with us."

He was the practical type. He drew his revolver and waved us towards their car. He must have

48

been about five foot five in his stockinged feet. Rocha stood up and gave him a withering look.

"Think you're a man with that shooter in your hand, don't you?" he said, spitting onto the grass.

Seeing the youngster get out his gun, an older man, thin and exhausted, emerged from the car. "What's going on?" he asked, waving a sub-machine gun that dangled from his arm like a deformed hand.

"They're trying to be smart," said Tiny Tim.

"Are you drunk or something? They're here to perform. Come on, leave them alone."

The trio moved off. Suddenly the small guy turned and smashed Rocha's left hand with his metal gun butt. The big fellow doubled over, clutching at his fingers.

"Let's see you lead with your left now," his tormentor smirked.

They climbed into their car and drove slowly away. Fatso, resting his elbow on an open window, poked his head out and shouted: "Remember, Golden Voice, you owe me an autograph."

I went over to Rocha. Blood was trickling from between the knuckles of his left hand. He clenched and unclenched his fist, gritting his teeth and breathing hard through the nose. He looked at me without asking for any pity or showing any signs of reproach. "Give me a cigarette," he said.

CHAPTER SIX

I wrapped some ice cubes in a towel and Rocha pressed it on his injured hand. He leaned back against the headboard with his legs stretched out on the mattress. He asked me to take his shoes off. He wore size twelve, but the shoes were so tight I had to prise them off with a spoon. The landlady sold me two beers, and while we were sipping them I tried to convince him the best thing would be to catch the night train back to Buenos Aires. But the worse the swelling grew, the more stubborn he became.

"Pride doesn't come into it," I insisted. "You're not fit to fight; any doctor will tell you that. And as for me, if the police beat up a colleague I refuse to sing even if they pay me double."

"If you're shitting yourself that's your problem. I'm going to fight. Nobody treats me like that."

"Listen to me, will you?"

"Save your breath. You quit if you want to. Leave the money for the room and clear out. I'm staying - I'll take on the lot of them if I have to. You think I don't know what's going on? The

50

slogan and then those thugs to scare me off. It's the oldest trick in the book. It's always the same in these hick towns..."

I was going to try to explain when there was a knock at the door. Before I could get up, Aguila Bayo came in, together with a guy with fair hair and a moustache who was wearing a dark suit. Aguila Bayo seemed agitated, and when he saw Rocha on the bed a look of regret stole over his face.

"You don't know how sorry I am about this, champ," he said, rushing over to inspect Rocha's hand. "You must go straight to the hospital. They'll give you a couple of pills and tomorrow you'll be back in top form. Come on, the inspector's car is outside."

"And afterwards we'll go to the station to take your statement," the other man said. "Before you two leave we'll catch those bastards."

"They said they were the police," I noted.

He glowered at me, then smiled. "The old story. Anybody with a gun can claim to be a policeman, and then the force's reputation stinks. But we're putting a stop to all that. I can assure you that by tomorrow they'll be arrested. I've put the whole unit on the job."

"See?" said Rocha. "It's all a campaign to put me off, so their kid can catch me demoralised. I wasn't born yesterday, you know."

"That's right," Aguila Bayo enthused. "That's

why you must do your utmost to defend your unbeaten record."

"Well, I'm not exactly unbeaten," Rocha said. "They tried the same trick in Villa Maria and stole the fight from me. That's why I said I've seen it all."

He spat into the gap between the bed and the wall. I looked at the man with the moustache, who was standing there stiffly to attention.

"Are you the inspector?" I asked, sitting back in my chair.

"Yes. Inspector Baltierrez."

"Who painted those slogans on the wall?" I asked.

He looked at me with the same expression as the fat man when I refused to sign my autograph. Eventually he replied:

"Kids, delinquents, some idiot who as usual is against everything that's being done for the town. But for your peace of mind I can assure you that there are very few of their kind left, and now all they can do is to daub on walls." He smiled, and went on confidentially, "A sad thing to be painting slogans attacking popular idols, don't you think?"

"Almost as sad as to be guarding the theatre with a group of thugs who attack people with a revolver to get their autograph."

He plunged his hands in his pockets and came over to my chair. He stopped so close that the clasp on his belt was nearly brushing my nose.

"You're nervous, Señor Galvan," he informed me.

"Very nervous," said Aguila Bayo, dabbing at his forehead with a handkerchief. "It's understandable isn't it, Inspector, after the fright they had?"

He tucked his handkerchief away and turned to Rocha, "Champ, put your shoes on and we'll get you to the hospital."

"It's not serious," Rocha grumbled. "Nothing's broken."

"That doesn't matter," the lawyer said. "I'll feel better once Dr Furlari has had a look at you. He is going to be the fight doctor as well."

He picked up Rocha's shoes and handed them to him. "Here you are. Hurry up."

Rocha appealed to me with eyes like those of a thrashed puppy. While I was putting his shoes on, the inspector checked his watch a couple of times, and Aguila Bayo said in a tone that brooked no contradiction: "And then you're coming to my house so I can look after you until it's time for the fight."

"No, I'm fine here with my friend..."

"Friends are the least of it." He was emphatic: "First and foremost come your sport and your duty to the public. Señor Galvan won't worry about having to spend a night alone. After the fight you can do as you please, but before it I'm sorry, but I'm taking charge of you. You have to be in shape for the weighing-in."

Rocha watched as Aguila Bayo picked up his

bag. He wanted to protest, but was too worried about his hand, which by now had swollen to the size of a guitar.

"Come and visit," Rocha said to me. "If you decide to stay and want to see me before the fight, I've already forgiven you for what you said, so..."

"Thanks," I replied. "I'll come and see you tomorrow. And take care, they reckon the local kid is hot stuff..."

He straightened my tie with his good hand. "I'll dump him in the third." He took out a large banknote and stuck it into my top pocket with a flourish. "Pay for the room and let me have the change later."

They left. Before closing the door, the inspector turned to me and asked, challenging: "Who was it who contracted you?"

"Captain Suarez," I replied, stressing the *Captain.*

He shut the door a little too violently.

I was hungry. I asked the landlady to fix me a sandwich, then settled down for a siesta.

At about five in the afternoon someone banged on my door with something heavier than a fist. I woke with a start, got my trousers on, and opened up. If my national service memories were correct, standing there were a top sergeant and a tall thin private who was nonchalantly holding his rifle barrel.

"Andres Galvan," the sergeant said.

"Yes."

"You're to come with me."

I went to put my shirt and shoes on. The sergeant and the soldier came into the room and peered into all the corners.

"Where are we going?" I asked.

"To headquarters."

I didn't like the idea, but it was no time to argue. Five minutes later we climbed into their jeep. The landlady followed us to the front door without a word, but she made sure I wasn't taking my suitcase with me. We had to pass through three checkpoints, where we were searched as if my escort were complete strangers. They stopped the jeep a hundred yards from each barrier; the three of us got out and stood in the middle of the road while the sergeant shouted who we were and where we were going. A warrant officer and a private came up, checked our documents, the jeep itself, and my pockets. At the final guardpost, when we'd been through the whole rigmarole, the officer on duty said to the sergeant, "How's things, Carrizo?"

They left me in a big room with four conscripts sitting on wooden benches. Every time I took out my cigarettes they swarmed around me to get their hands on one, but they put them straight into their pockets without a word. An hour later, a fair-haired soldier came in and told me to follow him. He showed me into an office decorated with portraits of all our military heroes from San Martin on, except for Peron.

Captain Suarez was in fatigues. His boots were polished as though for the cinema. He had rolled his sleeves up, and his broad chest bulged out of his shirt. He was a little over forty, with the kind of face well suited to his job. Beside him sat a smiling, impeccably groomed man I knew from television.

"Señor Morales," the Captain introduced him.

I shook hands. Morales said, "How are you? It's been years since we met" (stressing the *years*), then sat down again. There was no chair for me, so I stood next to the desk. Suarez settled back in his seat, shook a finger at me to show he was doing his duty as a concerned officer, and announced, "Unfortunately, Señor Galvan, your performance in Colonia Vela has had to be suspended."

I said nothing, waiting for him to go on.

"I'll be frank with you," he said. "When we contracted you, we were unaware that you had been...," he searched for the word, "...exempted from television immediately after the military government was formed."

I looked over at Morales, who was nodding agreement. He had been working in television for fifteen years without trouble from anyone; some people even said he was "an honest man".

"Might I know the reason?" the captain asked.

56

"I never did," I told him. "Perhaps as you're a member of the armed forces you can tell me."

He lit a cigarette. I was still standing there like a schoolboy being punished. "Permit me to remind you that the only people not allowed to appear were either terrorists or people involved in financial corruption."

"Which category did I come under?" I wanted to know.

"We have no evidence against you as regards financial matters," he said, flicking through a folder on the desk in front of him. I'd have given anything to have a look at it myself. Instead I stared at the photograph of the president hanging behind Captain Suarez.

"Are you insinuating I'm a terrorist, Captain?"

"I'm not insinuating anything," he said angrily. "If I want to say something I say it straight out. Did you do your national service?"

"Yes sir, in the First Army Corps."

"Then you'll know that an army man's word is his bond."

He stood up suddenly, pushing the chair back noisily. He must have rehearsed it, because he did it rather well. "Señor Galvan," he said. "Aguila Bayo will pay you your fee since I promised it and my promise is as good as any contract, but I advise you to return to Buenos Aires tonight."

He sat down again and concluded: "Good afternoon."

Morales made no attempt to say goodbye. I went out to the corridor where the fair-haired conscript was waiting.

"How do I get back into town?" I asked.

"I'll report to the sergeant," he said, and went off to find him.

We passed back through the three checkpoints and then they dropped me off near the station.

CHAPTER SEVEN

Dusk was drawing on by the time I reached the boardinghouse. As I crossed the patio the landlady came out to tell me that some gentlemen had been there asking after me. The door to the room was open. They had searched my suitcase and hadn't bothered to put anything back. The bed was in a mess, the mattress spilled on to the floor. I called the landlady.

"It was three armed men. They've been here before; whenever someone new arrives in town they come to have a look. The way things are, you can't be too careful, can you?"

I paid for the room. She told me the train for Buenos Aires left at 22.35, so I quickly packed my suitcase. I had a couple of hours to say goodbye to Rocha, get my money off Aguila Bayo, and have something to eat. I left my case with the landlady and went out about eight-thirty. The streets were empty; when I reached the square I saw workmen busy setting up lights and the stands for the celebrations which were to start the next day. On the same wall where that morning someone had painted the slogans against us, two soldiers had just finished pasting up a poster that announced:

TONY ROCHA
CONTENDER FOR THE NATIONAL TITLE
vs
MARCIAL SEPULVEDA
UNBEATEN HOPE OF COLONIA VELA
SUNDAY AT 10 PM IN THE
UNION AND PROGRESS CLUB
THE PEOPLE AND ITS ARMED FORCES
UNITED IN A COMMON DESTINY
OF PEACE AND GLORY

Five yards further on there was another poster:

THE CORRALES BROTHERS'
FAMOUS CIRCUS
ACROBATS CLOWNS WILD ANIMALS
MONDAY 6 PM ON THE SITE OF THE
FORMER BUILDING WORKERS' UNION
MASTER OF CEREMONIES:
JORGE OMAR MORALES
THE PEOPLE AND ITS ARMED FORCES
UNITED IN A COMMON DESTINY
OF PEACE AND GLORY

A theatre employee was busy removing the last poster from its notice board:

ONLY APPEARANCE BY
ANDRES GALVAN
BUENOS AIRES' GOLDEN VOICE
MONDAY 10 PM AVENUE THEATRE

THE PEOPLE AND ITS ARMED FORCES
UNITED IN A COMMON DESTINY
OF PEACE AND GLORY

A youth in overalls was improvising another poster in black letters on a yellow background:
GRAND CONCERT BY
CARLOS ROMERO
THE VELVET VOICE OF COLONIA VELA
MONDAY 10 PM AVENUE THEATRE
THE PEOPLE AND ITS ARMED FORCES
UNITED IN A COMMON DESTINY
OF PEACE AND GLORY

The boy didn't have enough room for the last sentence so he began to squash up all the letters from the word *Common* on.

Romero was finally getting his chance. It might be the last of his life, but he'd never forget it. I saw him coming out of the theatre with two other men, both taller than he but no younger. It was obvious they were delighted.

"Galvan, my friend!" Romero shouted, coming over to me. He shook hands, pumping my arm. A look of concern flitted across his face. "I got a call just now," he said. "They told me you weren't well...your throat, is it?"

I nodded in confirmation.

"You ought to take care," he said, laying a cautionary finger on my chest, "it's a risky business, especially at these changes of season. But don't worry, the prestige of the tango is safe in my hands. I hope you'll be in the front row, because I'm going to dedicate *South* to you."

"Thanks, but I'm afraid I have to leave tonight."

"Shame," and he seemed genuinely upset, "a real shame. Where can I send you a recording of the concert? We're going to tape it, you know."

"Aguila Bayo will forward it to me. Thanks a lot."

I shook hands again and crossed the square. Outside the town hall they were putting the finishing touches to a stand decorated in the national sky-blue and white. A black Torino stood outside the bar, its rear door open on the pavement side. The bar door was suddenly flung open, and a guy built like a wardrobe, a gun in his left hand, came out dragging a kid of around sixteen by the hair. He yanked him up, and then hit him with his gun in the small of the back so that he toppled into the back of the car. The big guy stowed the revolver in his belt and pushed his way in beside him. The car sped off and disappeared down the street. No one came out of the bar; no one inside looked out of the windows. I had been thinking of having something to eat, but suddenly I realised I wasn't hungry. I went in to have a coffee at the bar. About ten of the tables were occupied; everyone stared at me as I pushed open the door. They had all stopped talking, but as soon as they heard me order a coffee a hum of conversation started up again. The bar owner greeted me, but without a smile. He must have remembered it was me who had invited the tramp to sit down that morning. I asked what had been going on, but he pretended not to hear me; he turned to pick up the spirit measure and a bottle of whiskey and said, "A double?"

I said no thanks, but didn't repeat my question. To be on the safe side, he kept well away from me.

I had finished my coffee and left the money for it on the bar when Aguila Bayo came in. He was with a stocky, hard-faced man wearing a zipped-up jacket baggy enough to conceal all the weapons of the First Army Corps. Aguila Bayo pretended he hadn't seen me; he greeted people at a couple of tables, then went to sit at the window. His companion made his way to the back of the bar and sat where he had a good view of the door and the lawyer. He didn't take his eyes off me as I went over to Aguila Bayo's table, not even when a broad-hipped blonde brushed past him and beat me to it. I hesitated a moment, but I was already on my way, so I went up to the two of them, and said, "I'm sorry, but I have to talk to you."

The blonde lit a cigarette and stared into space. As usual, Aguila Bayo was wearing a suit, vest, and a bow tie. His hair was slicked back impeccably. Only the cane was missing.

"I haven't the time now," he said, underlining my impertinence. "Come and see me at midday tomorrow."

"I have to leave tonight," I told him.

He stared at me, then smiled. "Tonight? Aren't you going to stay for the celebrations?"

"You know very well I'm not."

"I do? I don't know anything, my friend. All I was told was that you were indisposed and that I should find a stand-in."

He was displaying his hypocrisy openly, and I realised it wasn't going to be easy to get my money out of him. "Captain Suarez said to see you, and to make sure I left today."

He chuckled, and took a cigarette from the blonde's pack. "You know what these army people are like. They love giving orders, but there's a big gap between saying and doing. Come and see me tomorrow."

I was growing impatient. "I've already left the boardinghouse."

"Go back there. They always have rooms available."

I sat down without asking. "Listen to me." I tried to look threatening: "There're a few things I have to talk to you about, either on our own or here, whichever you prefer."

He glanced at the blonde, who seemed to be telling him to get rid of this jerk.

"Come with me," he said, moving to another

table.

I sat down opposite him.

"You didn't perform," he said for starters.

"But there was an agreement, and I didn't break it."

"Nor did I," he said, offended. "The idea came from above."

"From Captain Suarez," I said. "I was with him this afternoon."

"No, higher up than that," he said, lowering his voice. "From intelligence..."

It was his turn to try to scare me.

"Aha? And how do you know that?"

He smiled, full of himself, arrogant, as though giving me a glimpse of his ace of spades.

"I even know the colour of your shorts."

The blood rushed to my head. "You like rummaging in other people's cases, don't you?"

He laughed in my face. Then he straightened his bow tie and looked at me; now he was showing me his ace openly. "I don't do the dirty work, Galvan."

I had to agree. The blonde was alternating her attention between her watch and our table.

"We're all dying to hear you," he went on, "but orders are orders."

"Yeah, and it's always been my life's ambition to sing in Colonia Vela. That'll have to wait, but for now you owe me..."

He interrupted me: "Don't be vulgar, Galvan: I don't owe you anything. After all, it was the army who contracted you, wasn't it?"

He wasn't the type to scare easily. Worse still, he was rude about it.

"Look, I was contracted by someone called Suarez who got in touch with my agent in Buenos Aires. Now Suarez tells me to get my money and leave today. And you are the person he says should pay me. Is that clear enough?"

"It's not that simple. I need the captain's written authorisation."

"You ask him for it," I said, pointing to the telephone. He grinned, revealing an uneven set of teeth with one gold cap.

"Do you think you can phone army headquarters as if it were the cinema?"

"OK. How do we settle this then?"

"If you insist on leaving tonight, I'll send you a check for the money tomorrow...you surely don't think I would keep something that isn't mine, do you?"

"I don't think anything. What if I don't go?"

He leaned back in his chair, glanced sideways at his blonde companion, then stared down at his own dainty hands. "I like you, you know that? You seem decent enough. You signed a few appeals, you said some political rubbish on the radio, and because you're a bit innocent you sang in the odd youth festival. You know terrorism is like a red

66

flag to these people. They don't make any distinctions. Or maybe they do, and pay too much attention to details; I don't know. They're well-intentioned, they want to drag this country out of a mess; and if you behave, they know how to forget."

He lowered his voice again as if to confide in me. "Take me, for example." He stubbed himself in the chest with his thumb. "I defended political prisoners in Azul, in 1971. Youngsters in it up to here, friend - yet look at me now."

"How many of them did you get off?"

"That's not the point. I stuck my neck out for what I believed was right at the time. I even have a letter from Peron thanking me. Things are different now. I've never been a Peronist, but he knew a thing or two. If they'd listened to him, none of this would have happened. But no, they reckoned they were more Peronist than Peron, and now look...the revolution!" He smiled indulgently. "They thought they only had to wish it to make it happen...then these people came along and sorted things out."

I had no idea why he was telling me all this. There was three quarters of an hour before my train left, and here we were, wasting time.

"Not to mention that other lot," he went on. "Those operetta bolsheviks who used toddlers in diapers to attack military barracks. There's not one of them left..."

"I don't go for political speeches in bars," I said.

He flashed his gold tooth again. He motioned to the blonde, who by now was squirming in her seat as though she had ants in her pants, and said to me drily: "Do as you wish. If you leave, I'll send you the check. If you stay, I'll give you a ticket for the fight."

"Thanks," I said. "I think I'll be going tonight. How is Rocha?"

He stood up and smiled at the girl. "He's fine. The doctor says all he needs is an injection. That boy is as strong as an ox."

"I'd like to say goodbye to him."

"I wouldn't recommend it. He's sleeping the sleep of the just. Martha is keeping an eye on him; he's well looked after, believe me. I'll say goodbye for you."

He went over to sit with his blonde friend, and I realised he must have said something about me because she gave me the dirtiest look imaginable. When the waiter came over, I said I was already leaving. Outside, a light drizzle had begun to fall, which barely wet the pavement but which forced me to turn my collar up. I went back to the boardinghouse to collect my case. I walked close to the walls to protect myself from the rain, and didn't see a soul the whole way. The landlady was eating a steak and salad when I showed up. She gave me my case and even raised a smile when we said our farewells. I had twenty-five minutes to reach the station, and the rain was too fine to scare me off. I was still sticking close to the walls; as I passed people's windows I could hear their TVs or a snatch of incomprehensible conversation. Everyone's blinds were drawn. I had reached the corner and was on the point of crossing the station forecourt when I heard a voice calling me. I couldn't work out where it came from. I stopped, lit a cigarette, and looked surreptitiously over at the waste lot. As a precaution, I took a few steps along the sidewalk out of the corner lamplight. The tramp's voice was telling me it was him, in among the trees and bushes of the lot. I could only just make him out, standing there with his coat buttoned up and wearing a hat against the rain. He was holding something in his right hand.

"Come and have a drink of *maté* with me," he said, almost in a whisper.

"I can't, I'll miss the train."

He took a step forward, took a sip of *maté* and looked over at the light from the streetlamp. "It's not heavy rain, but it's coming down steady," he commented.

"Aha."

"Don't let them see you," he said. "Leave your case where it is, go around the corner and come in here from the next street."

I didn't understand a thing, but I dropped my suitcase.

"Come on," he urged me. "Start walking before

69

they notice you!"

I avoided the pool of light, walked slowly around the corner, and flattened myself against a tree. The Falcon was drawn up outside the station entrance. I remembered the fat guy who had asked for my autograph in the square, and Gary Cooper on his high heels. Suddenly I was terrified; a childish terror full of shadows and silences. The hobo appeared out of the bushes.

"They didn't spot you," he said. "I got your case. Follow me."

As he pushed aside the damp undergrowth it brought back distant memories of how as a kid I used to hide with my friends in places like this, where we'd whisper secrets to each other, smoke bitter-tasting leaves without inhaling, and all of us dream about the bicycle repair man's wife.

The hut the tramp had built from scrap also reminded me of those we made as kids. It must have been impossible to spot in the summer, when the greenery completely concealed it; and it had the same welcoming air, apart from the sour smell of dirt, tobacco and rotten fruit. A dark-coloured mattress and a blanket that had once been brown lay on the earthen floor. The other furniture consisted of two crates, one a table and the other a chair, where the tramp sat before adding water to his *maté*. The one luxury item, absurdly out of place, was a small gas stove. Laid out on top of an oil drum were two lighted candles, a packet of *maté* tea, sugar, a knife, and some other objects I couldn't bring myself to investigate too closely. The tramp picked up a loaf of bread from one of the wooden crates and waved his hand for me to sit down. I stared at him; he handed me a frothy hot *maté* and the first swallow brought back feeling to my body. The rain was caressing the leaves outside; the perfume that wafted in made it almost pleasant to breathe inside the hut.

"I don't think I asked you your name this morning," I said.

"Oh, no one asks me that," he said with a laugh, "I'm not used to formal introductions."

I smiled and handed back the *maté.*

"Luciano," he said; "Luciano Melencof, or Maleancof, I can't remember which. I haven't used my real name in years. Everybody calls me Mingo."

"How did you find out?" I asked, jerking my head in the direction of the station.

"They paid me a visit, to ask me what we had been talking about this morning, and then they parked over there."

"But why?" I said, asking myself the question.

He handed me another *maté.* "They haven't got so much to do these days. So they ask questions, select. When the train leaves and they realise you aren't on it, they're going to turn nasty. And that fat man is evil, no mistake."

"So you know them well?"

71

"They shot three kids right in front of me, against the wall back there. The kids were already a mess, but before they finished them off they really went to town on them."

I was trying to hide my fear, but it almost got the better of me. I sucked hard at the *maté* to choke back my impulse to vomit.

I passed him the *maté* and he put it on the oil drum.

"Here's what we'll do. Once they've gone we'll cross the railway tracks and head for open country. If you walk all night you should reach Tandil by morning. You can get a bus to Buenos Aires from there."

We sat in silence. Then we heard the train leave. Two minutes later everything was quiet again. Then we heard a car skidding around the corner on the wet asphalt. I was about to breathe a sigh of relief when another car, with a quieter, more discreet, engine pulled up by the waste ground.

CHAPTER EIGHT

The tramp raised a finger to his lips in a gesture that was more instinctive than a sign of fear that I would make a noise. One of the car doors opened, and someone shouted, "Hey, Mingo!"

Frozen with cold and terror, I watched Mingo struggle to his feet. I was thinking that if he didn't get outside quickly, they would investigate the shack; I was also thinking he might give me away. He undid his filthy coat and took it off. The same voice, closer this time, called again: "Come on out, will you?"

Mingo gestured for me to stay close to the wall, and blew out the candles. Then he pushed one arm back into his raincoat, lifted the sacking at the hut entrance, and went out. I pressed my face against a slit and could see Mingo pushing his way through the bushes, at the same time struggling to put his coat on completely. The car headlights cut two swathes through the darkness, picking out the fine, drifting rain.

"I was asleep," Mingo said in what sounded to me like a defiant voice.

"Did you see him again?" asked the fat man, who now was wearing a dark sweater.

"See who?" Mingo said irately, stopping before he reached the pavement.

"Who?" the fat man shouted. "That tango singer from Buenos Aires, of course!"

"No," Mingo said.

"Have you been near the square?"

"What's that?"

"Wake up! I said, have you been anywhere near the square?"

"When?" Mingo was taking it too far. I thought Fatso had his eyes on the shack, and shrank back against the wall.

"Stop trying to be smart," he said, and stepped into the waste lot.

"I was asleep, dammit," Mingo grunted, turning his back. The fat man didn't come any further, and finally shouted with a laugh, "One of these days we'll set fire to all these bushes and clear out your pigsty while we're at it."

Mingo came back into the hut; the fat man climbed into his car. It sped off towards the town centre. Mingo began scrabbling around on the floor for his matches. I lit the candles with my lighter.

"What time is it?" he asked me.

"Ten forty-five."

"It's time we set off across country. I'll go with

74

you as far as the brothel, then I'll show you the way. If you keep going you'll reach Tandil by morning, and from there you can catch the bus."

He put his hat on and went over to the doorway. "If there's anything you need in your case, get it now. We'll leave the case in the bushes; when I get back I'll bury it."

I opened it and took out my black jacket and a book I'd got halfway through on the train. For some reason before I put it back in the case I unfolded the last page I had read. Mingo watched me with respect.

"My father used to read a lot," he said.

Then he went to the far end of the waste ground, and I could barely make out his dark outline as he hid the case in among the bushes. I put the jacket on over the one I was wearing. It was a tight fit, but at least it would protect me from the drizzle. Mingo went to the street, looked both ways, and crossed. From the opposite sidewalk he motioned for me to follow him. We made a detour to avoid the station and crossed the tracks, running towards a goods van that was hooked forever to a rusty locomotive. We crouched down by its wheels and for some reason crawled underneath, though it would have been much easier to walk around it. A dark horizon opened in front of us, in which all I could see was one of those large sheds you find in all railway stations. The rain was soaking my clothes, and when I ran my hand through my hair I realised it was a mess, falling all over my ears. We slipped through a fence and found ourselves in a field of oats. When I looked back, I saw that the lights of the town were being blotted out by the rainy gloom. I wasn't scared any more. The further we got from the lights, the more easily I could breathe, and in the darkness and silence of the fields I felt I was coming alive again.

After another hour's walking, the cold was paralysing my legs, and I had a bitter taste in my mouth. I rested against a tree to light a cigarette. Mingo, who was walking a few yards ahead, stopped when he saw the lighter flame. He trudged back to me and I handed him a cigarette. He fished a bottle of gin out of his coat pocket and took what seemed like an endless swig; then he passed it to me and we sat slumped on the wet ground by the tree to drink. We exchanged the bottle three or four times. A cricket began to chirrup close by. Mingo pointed to somewhere in among the vegetation.

"There's luck, friend," he said. "You're going to be lucky."

I watched him bend the elbow again. Finally, he lowered the bottle and gave it to me.

"That cricket," he said. "When they sing it means good luck."

"They always sing. That's what they're there for, isn't it?"

"It's easy to tell you're a city boy," Mingo said, disappointed.

The cricket chirruped again, this time loud and uninterrupted. Mingo got to his knees, put an ear to the ground, then shuffled off into the undergrowth. He felt around in the greenery, and suddenly the cricket fell silent. When the tramp returned, he was holding it carefully in his closed fist. I lit my lighter to get a look. Mingo clasped it gently in his fingers. The insect thrashed its long back legs as Mingo passed it to me.

"Be careful, the legs are the weakest part."

I took hold of it carefully; the cricket tickled my fingers as it searched for a gap to wriggle through. I cupped both hands together to give it room. Once again I had the feeling I was going back in time, back to my childhood. Except that now there was no one to tell my adventure to.

"OK," Mingo said. "Let's go."

I opened my fingers and the cricket jumped out, invisible to me. A brief sensation of emptiness clung to my hands.

I followed him. To his back I muttered all that had happened to Rocha and myself during the day. I was more or less talking to myself, because Mingo was some way ahead, pushing his way through the vegetation and dodging to avoid pot-holes. He didn't say a word until I had finished.

"Why wouldn't you give him your autograph?"

I walked on in silence for a while, then said, "Would you have signed it?"

He stopped, turned around, and seemed to be gazing at some distant point in the darkness. Then he lowered his gaze and scuffed the ground with his foot. Either he was thinking, or he was taking time to answer. Eventually he said, "I don't know. Each to his own. Do I look like someone who goes around signing autographs?"

The rain had brought a chill breeze with it. Some way off I could see the outline of a big shed. I reckoned we could rest up there a while and perhaps light a fire to dry our clothes. We slipped through another wire fence and had to walk around a corn field. This brought us out into an open grassy patch which led to the shed. By its entrance I could see the blackened, twisted remains of the frame of a small aircraft. Weeds had overgrown its wheels and were pushing their way into the pilot's cockpit. The door, hanging from one hinge, had at least twenty round holes in it, each one as thick as a finger. A few yards further on, by a clump of willows, two wooden crosses stuck out of the earth.

I took all this in with the kind of vague curiosity you feel on entering a cemetery. I bent over the crosses. Even though I shielded it in my hands, the lighter went out several times before I could read the names inscribed in uneven lettering on the wood. I walked back to the plane and sheltered beneath the rusty struts of one of the wings. Mingo trampled down the weeds to walk over to the cockpit, and peered inside as if looking for something he'd mislaid long ago. He didn't move for a while, but stood there with the upper half of his body inside the plane. When finally he straightened up, his hat brushed the fuselage and fell into the grass. He shook it, put it back on, then came and crouched next to me. He tapped my arm for another cigarette, and pointed to the crosses.

"The army people got tired of pulling them up and finding somebody always put them back, so in the end they left them where they were."

I recalled Romero's story. Mingo got out the bottle, put it to his lips, and tilted his head back until he was convinced that it really was empty. He threw it against the hangar wall.

"Oh, shit," he said.

We smoked for a while in silence. I was thinking how absurd it was to run away like this, and pictured myself all alone in the middle of the countryside, walking for hours through the rain to arrive at the next town an exhausted wreck, simply to get on a bus that would take me to Buenos Aires. How could I be sure that would be the end of it, once I was far enough away from Fatso and Gary Cooper? Would that file I'd seen on Captain Suarez's desk follow me to the capital? Suddenly I remembered Rocha. I couldn't get his flattened nose and orang-utan physique out of my mind.

Unconsciously, I felt in my pocket for the bank-note he had given me. It was too much - I was sure he couldn't have any more money with him. I played with the note between my fingers, folding it like a letter, until Mingo's voice snapped me out of myself.

"We ought to be getting a move on." He took a last drag on his cigarette, stubbed it out on the ground, and stood up. "Your luck is in," he said, pointing to the banknote.

That made me laugh. Mingo laughed too, though his sounded forced. Then, without a trace of spite in his voice, he said, "They pay well, those army people."

I didn't say a word. I had a queasy feeling in the pit of my stomach, as if I had smoked too much. "It's Rocha's. He left it to pay for his room."

Mingo went back to the aircraft and peered into the cockpit again.

"That kid's on a hiding to nothing," he announced casually, the words seeming to roll around inside the aircraft carcass before reaching me. Then he began to pull creepers off the propeller.

"I've already told him that," I said.

I sat slumped on the ground with my back against the fuselage, listening to the rain and his heavy breathing. I didn't feel like going on. I couldn't face it. Beyond the grass field there was nothing. I put the note back into my pocket.

"Is Sepulveda that good then?"

Mingo was sitting in the cabin, his legs dangling over the side. All I could see of him was his hat.

"He's very quick," he said. "And they aren't going to let him lose on the day of the town celebrations, are they? They've been keeping him shut up in the barracks, getting him to work out with punchbag and skipping rope every day."

"In the barracks?"

"Where else? They've even brought in a sparring partner from Mendoza. They make sure he's seen around town, so everybody gets a good look at the state of his face after the army boy's been at him."

"Is Sepulveda doing his army service then?"

Mingo stood up and peered at me over the top of the aircraft door. "Are you being funny?"

"Why?"

"Didn't you know he's a lieutenant?"

"Sepulveda?"

He sat down again, and I heard him say, "I thought you were sharper than that, friend."

I sat thinking, trying to take it in, trying to work out the link between Sepulveda being an army officer and the concern Aguila Bayo and his daughter were showing for our orang-utan friend. "Rocha doesn't suspect a thing."

"What does he care?" Mingo said. "He knows he's for it. He'll make a few bucks out of it...if he's smart, he'll take a dive at the right moment."

"He doesn't know a thing. He thinks he's going to win for sure."

Mingo laughed at the idea, clambered down and bummed another cigarette. "If only we had some more gin...d'you think we can make a move now?"

"We have to warn him."

"Warn him? He'll find out tomorrow."

"D'you reckon they smashed his hand in on purpose?"

He spread his arms wide. "I dunno. I can't see it. Why would they risk the fight being postponed?"

"If only Rocha had two good hands..."

Mingo laughed again, but this time with a hollow sound. "Don't be stupid, Galvan, there's no way he can win. That would be a kick up the arse for the whole army, wouldn't it?"

My legs had gone to sleep. I stood up and hobbled over to the willows. "We have to go back," I said.

"You want to go back to town?"

"I want to talk to Rocha. Anyway, I have to give him his money back."

"It won't do any good," he said. "For now, they just want to give you a good working over, but if you start stirring things up, you're done for. They don't believe in half measures, you know."

He stood there staring at me; I think he was

pleased I was staying. He slapped the aircraft fuselage and said, with a new edge to his voice, "Let's move, then. We can go back by the brothel for a bottle. This cold has got into my bones. How d'you feel?"

CHAPTER NINE

When we caught sight of the four soldiers standing guard outside the whorehouse, we ducked behind a clump of bushes. They were huddled against the walls, swathed in plastic capes. A song by Leonardo Favio drifted on the wind from inside the building.

"If there's soldiers that means the army's having a night out," Mingo said. "It must be the NCOs - when it's the officers, they block off the road and bring the whole regiment to guard the place."

"Who runs it?" I asked.

"The lawyer."

"Aguila Bayo?"

Mingo's expression again showed he thought I must have been born yesterday.

"D'you reckon he's in there?" I asked him.

"He must be. He's never far from the military."

"I have to make sure."

He stared at me. He was waiting for me to tell him what I had to make sure of.

"I have to know if he's there or not. Then I can go and see Rocha while he's on his own."

"Maybe he brought him along."

"I don't think so. That would be going too far."

"You reckon?" His eyes mocked me.

I was beginning to feel worried. If Rocha was in the brothel, I'd have to find some way of getting him out without the lawyer noticing.

"Do the soldiers know you?"

"I'm not exactly famous, but I think most of them know me by sight."

"Could you keep them talking for me?"

"What am I supposed to tell them? That I'm out for a breath of fresh air?"

"Tell them anything, while I have a look inside."

Mingo scanned the brightly lit house, the cars, a jeep parked over by a line of poplars, and the soldiers patrolling close by the wall, their machine guns slung from their shoulders.

"I'll have to scout round by the trees and come down the road. I hope they recognise me, or they'll shoot first and ask questions later."

"Will you do it or won't you?"

"Do I have any choice?"

He trotted off alongside the fence until I lost sight of him. A few minutes later, I heard a whistle from somewhere down the road. I walked to the fence, peeled off my soaked jacket, and crawled through the wires. I sat crouched in the ditch for a while. The rain was making enough noise to cover any sound my feet made on the twigs. I crept along until I could hide behind a car. A soldier shouted: "Halt!"

He jumped out to the road, machine gun at the ready. Another of the guards came to take up position behind the same car I was sheltering against. I held my breath; the soldier pushed something on his machine gun which gave a sharp click, then propped it on the front of the car. He seemed too intent on what he was doing to realise I was only a yard from him. Suddenly the road was bathed in light, and I ducked down behind a wheel so he wouldn't spot me. Someone had switched the jeep headlights on. Mingo came sauntering through the puddles, waving his hat as if to a crowd.

"Don't shoot, dammit!" he shouted. Then he burst out laughing. The soldier close by me relaxed, and felt for a cigarette in his cape pocket. As he lit it, his face was suddenly illuminated, but too briefly for me to catch sight of his features. He threw the match down at my feet and emerged to confront Mingo.

I stole across the street behind the jeep. The four soldiers had surrounded Mingo. I could hear one of them asking, "What the fuck are you doing here?" as I entered the lighted yard that encircled the house. I tried to walk like just another client, and went up to one of the two open windows. D'Arienzo was singing now, and people were dancing. There can't have been more than fifteen women for forty or fifty drunken men. The ones without partners were jeering at the tango steps the others were attempting. I took in all the room, glancing over my shoulder now and then out of fear that somebody might recognise me. Aguila Bayo was sitting at a table, gesticulating at four men who were trying hard to stay awake. I checked everyone dancing - no Rocha. I did see the blonde Aguila Bayo had met in the café, and the sergeant who had come for me at the boardinghouse. By the bar, two drunks were struggling with a fat guy who wanted to pick a fight and was roaring like a bull. There wasn't enough room even to spit; at the back door a few bored-looking men couldn't decide whether it was better to go out for some fresh air and get wet or to stay inside and put up with the stench of tobacco and sweat. I walked around to the back yard as casually as I could. There were four rooms with closed doors; lights shone through their curtains. A table for about fifty people had been laid in the gallery which filled the whole width of the house; it was littered with empty bottles and dirty plates. Half a dozen men were still sitting there, listening to the night's final stories. A big barbecue, protected from the rain by iron sheeting, stood in the middle of the yard. Smoke still drifted from the coals. The door to one of the rooms opened and a dark-haired youth came out, pulling on his jacket. In a fit of politeness, he shook hands with the naked woman who was with him. The men at the table applauded, and one of them called out, "Get your oats, eh, Blackie?" Another jumped up, staggered, then zigzagged halfheartedly across to the room. Bathed in sweat, the woman stared up at the drizzle, then at me, and then closed the door again. The new arrival sat down at the table to a great round of back-slapping. He seemed less drunk than the rest.

I crossed the yard as far from the lights as I could, and headed for the gate. Mingo was talking to three of the soldiers beside the jeep. The fourth had climbed inside and was smoking a cigarette. They'd switched the headlights off. They didn't seem to be on the alert, so I slipped out onto the sidewalk hoping to get away as quietly as possible. I passed the first window without stopping to look in; the front door was ajar, and the voice of Miguel Montero singing *The Grandfather Clock* came clearly from inside. A bottle shattered the last window on the side of the house, and the pieces of glass smashed at my feet. The noise scared the wits out of me. I peered anxiously inside. Three drunks were manhandling the same loudmouth who'd been shouting at the bar earlier. Someone's hand closed on my shoulder.

"The fun's starting," a voice said.

I turned slowly around. The man took his hand away and finished doing up his fly. He had wet himself all down his left trouser leg.

"Yeah, the fun's started," he repeated, as if

speaking to himself.

I tried to walk on, but I hadn't gone two steps when he called, "Hey!"

He staggered up to me. He had a soft, plump face and needed a shave. "Give me a cigarette," he said.

I gave him one. He stared at me quizzically while searching through all his pockets for a match. I realised he was beginning to think he knew me.

"Have you been with fat Anna?" he jerked his head in the direction of the back yard.

Instead of replying, I gave him a light.

"You haven't?" he was full of himself. "You don't know what you're missing. She puts her legs up here," - he folded his arms across his chest and touched his shoulders - "then she starts to go and go," he shut his eyes and swayed with pleasure. He was caught up in his dream until I made a move to go. Then he came to and quizzed me again, this time quite openly.

"You're..."

"I have to be going," I said, foolishly.

This startled him. "Where are you off to? Didn't they say we'd all be leaving together?"

"I'm going for a piss, then I'll be back."

I set off into the darkness but it was no use. He came plodding after me.

"This'll do," he said. "Watch out for the wind."

I was so nervous it took me a long time to produce anything at all. Finally a thin stream trickled into the grass.

"I know you," he insisted. "I've seen you in...where was it I saw you?"

"In Azul?" I suggested.

Standing there in the darkness surrounded by weeds, he looked like the trunk of a tree struggling in a high wind. He watched me piss in silence. A gust which barely ruffled my hair knocked him back a couple of yards, but he wouldn't give up. He puffed on his cigarette and returned to the charge: "No, it can't have been Azul. I haven't been to Azul in years."

I did up my trousers and made for the side wall of the house. Nobody would be able to see me there, and I'd be out of the rain. I had to get rid of him.

"What's your name then?" I asked him.

"Sergeant Jonte. Don't you remember me?"

I took a chance. "From Tandil?"

"From Tandil," he roared, "the barracks there, under Major Farina..."

"Yeah, Major Farina..." There was already a link between us. "D'you remember?"

"Remember what?"

"Well,...Farina...some guy, eh?"

"Who are you then?"

"Vega...everyone calls me Veguita."

90

He scratched his head. "Veguita...it doesn't mean..."

"Well, they call me Blackie too."

"Blackie? Oh, that's right, you're Blackie, that's it. A corporal, aren't you?"

"A corporal."

He stepped out into the road and bawled: "Soldier!"

I broke into a sweat. I desperately wanted to vanish and leave him talking to himself, but I needed an excuse.

"Soldier!" he shouted again.

One of the privates on guard duty came towards us, halting with his legs spread wide and one hand on his machine gun. He flicked on a flashlight. "Who goes there?" he asked wearily.

"Sergeant Jonte. Go fetch me a beer, will you?"

The soldier came up and shone the light in our faces.

"Good evening to you, Sergeant sir," he said.

"Good evening," Jonte growled. "Go and get two beers, will you, kid?"

"I can't leave my post, Sergeant sir."

"Come off it, do as I say."

"I'm sorry, Sergeant sir."

"What d'you mean, sorry? I'll make you sorry in the morning if you don't do as I say!"

"You'll have to see the officer in charge, Sergeant sir. Permission to return to guard duty,

Sergeant sir."

The private turned on his heel and left us. Jonte cursed him a few times until his anger subsided, and stuffed his hands into his pockets.

"Germani is on duty, and he's got them shit scared, the poor kids," he said, trying to explain the recruit's refusal to help. I seized the opportunity:

"Why don't you go and get them?"

He looked annoyed.

"Why not you, fuck it?" he said, feeling for the stripes on my forearm. "You're the corporal, aren't you?"

I bent over close to him: "Yes," I whispered in his ear, "but I'm dying for a shit."

He looked at me and stifled a laugh.

"While I'm doing it, you get the two beers."

"OK," he agreed. As he reeled off, he shouted, "You want me to bring you some paper while I'm at it?"

"These weeds will do fine," I answered, heading out into the darkness.

I watched until he disappeared through the front door; then I checked where the guards were and sneaked across the road. I slipped back through the wire fence, found my other jacket, and squatted down to see if there was any sign of Mingo.

"Where did you get to?" a voice said behind

92

me.

I turned to face him. "So that's how you keep the soldiers talking, is it?"

"The big chief came and booted me out. Is Rocha in there?"

"No. He must be at Aguila Bayo's."

"So we're heading back to town?"

"If you'll come with me...We'll have to hurry before our lawyer friend gets home."

He looked at me as if I was a raving idiot. "You mean you want to get into the house? Can't it wait until tomorrow?"

"You reckon Aguila Bayo would let me talk to him? I have to take my chance now."

"Come off it. That house is under closer guard than the police station."

"Let's try at least."

Nearby, another cricket began to chirrup. Mingo smiled and patted my arm.

"Have it your own way; at least your luck's in."

CHAPTER TEN

We crawled back under the same goods van. The birds sheltering from the rain flapped and banged into the wheels and axles until they found their way out. We skirted the railway station and started down the road to the town centre. Fifty yards from Mingo's shack, we came to a halt and gazed up at the sky, where the first light of Sunday was filtering through.

"The parting of the ways?" I asked.

"Fat chance."

I glanced at my watch. A quarter after five. I took off the sodden black jacket and threw it away. We crossed the street. Mingo looked longingly towards his hut as we passed by.

"We could do with a few *matés,*" he said.

We trudged on. After walking so long on grass, slithering in the mud, puddles and gopher holes, it was a relief to be able to stride along the asphalt, and I warmed up again. When we reached the lawyer's street, Mingo stopped me with a warning hand on my chest. He sneaked a look around the corner.

"I thought so, dammit!"

I peered over his shoulder. A black Torino with one door open was parked outside Aguila Bayo's house. We propped ourselves against the wall, catching our breath. Finally, Mingo whispered to me, "We have to get in anyway, don't we?"

"Do you know the place?"

"I think there's some waste ground behind the house, where they knocked a building down last year."

He peeped around the corner again.

"They'll be suspicious if we go across together. You take the opposite side of the road. I'll go around the block further down. Find the waste lot and wait for me by the wall of Aguila Bayo's house."

I smiled at him. I took out my cigarettes and offered him one. As he shuffled off I asked, "Why are you doing this?"

He blew out smoke and shrugged. "The kid's in a tight spot, isn't he?"

He started down the street. I waited until he vanished around the corner, then crossed the road. I tried to walk as slowly as possible, keeping one eye on the lawyer's house. There was no change: the car, a leaden silence. As I passed opposite the car, its door slammed shut. I fought off a sudden desire to run. I was aware of the slightest sound: the first stirrings of the birds, my own footsteps. I counted them one by one until I reached the waste ground. It was full of weeds, stones, and broken bricks. I trod carefully through the wet vegetation, stumbling on the rubble, and finally came up against a wall. I hadn't the faintest idea whether I was opposite the right house. I sat down on some damp bricks, and realised I was shivering, and my chest hurt. The rain had stopped, and when I lifted my head I could see day was dawning among grey clouds. I wondered how I could wake Rocha up without alerting Martha and having her warn the men in the car. I wondered too how on earth I was going to convince him of my story.

Mingo had taken off his coat and hat. As soon as he reached me, he put them both back on again, as if the image of himself in them meant a lot to him.

"Any news?" he asked, but didn't wait for my reply. He carried three bricks to the wall, clambered onto them, and looked over.

"I reckon this is the one," he said. I took a stone over and climbed up beside him. As far as I could tell in the dim first light, the garden was well looked after, with a bed of roses and a peach tree that was just coming into blossom. I was worried there might be a guard dog, but Mingo was already trying to scale the wall. He wasn't up to this kind of gymnastics; his eyes bulged with the effort, and his right hand clung to the edge of the wall so savagely it seemed all the bones were about to pierce the skin. He got one elbow on top of the wall, lifted himself with a grunt, and flailed with his right leg. His shoe caught the top, flaked off a big piece of whitewash, then slid back down. For a second he hung in mid-air, but his arm couldn't support all his weight, and slowly his body toppled over backwards. He hit the top brick, and crumpled to the ground. I tried to grab him, but I was too late. His head cracked against the stone I had placed against the wall, then he lay flat out, arms and legs spread-eagled.

I knelt over him. He wasn't moving, but he was breathing like an asthmatic. His eyes had glazed over. I shook him gently. As his eyes focussed, they shone a warning that he could do perfectly well without any help from me. When I ran a hand through his white hair, my fingers felt warm and sticky. His chest was heaving as though something was galloping along inside it. He managed to move an arm, then flexed one of his legs. He raised himself on one elbow, scrabbled against the wall, and got to his knees. He stayed like that for a minute until his breathing calmed. I tried to help him to his feet, but again he refused. He used the wall to lever himself upright, then went in search of his hat, which had rolled over near a concrete girder with rusty iron bars sticking out of it.

"Come on," he said.

"You've hurt your head."

He touched the wound coolly, with a hint of pride, and faced the wall again. "We have to talk to the kid, don't we? Why are you just standing there?"

"Let's have a smoke first," I said.

He was still out of breath, and I was scared he might fall off again. We smoked our cigarettes slowly, watching the sky turn red and become deeper and deeper. Halfway through his cigarette, he threw it away and trod it out. Without a word, he climbed back up on the bricks and repeated his previous antics. I watched closely until he managed to sit astride the wall. Then we jumped down as quietly as possible into the garden, and crept over to the house. A passageway on the left led out to the street. I tiptoed as far as the iron gate, and looked for the car.

I could see the tips of two cigarettes glowing behind the misted-up windshield. I walked back, pressed against the side wall, watching where I put my feet, frightened the slightest noise might give us away. The shutters were closed on the two windows. I thought one must belong to the room where Rocha was asleep. I made my way to the back of the house. Mingo stood there looking nonplussed, one hand on the door handle. He signalled me over.

"The best way into a house is through the door," he muttered, and turned the handle gently. The door opened without a sound.

Mingo gestured to me "what now?" I whispered in his ear, "Take your shoes off."

"If the daughter wakes up she'll raise hell," he said.

A cock crowed in the next door yard, and was answered by another one in the distance. I clutched my shoes in one hand, and lit my lighter in the other. The kitchen was on the left, with its door open; on the right was a small room with an ironing board, a washing machine and a linen cupboard which filled the end wall. We crept along the corridor, stopping each time the lighter burned my fingers and I had to blow it out. The only sound in the darkness was our breathing; the smell of our damp clothes filled my nostrils.

The corridor led into the entrance hall, with Aguila Bayo's study off to one side. On the other were two rooms with closed doors. I hesitated for a second, then on an impulse chose the one on the right. I brought my lighter close to the door knob, and turned it as slowly as possible. I pushed the door open gently, and held the lighter up. The flame flickered, then straightened and gave a dim view of the room. The bed was dishevelled and empty. Rocha's bag was open on a chair. I told Mingo what I'd seen.

"He must be at the whorehouse then," he sighed.

It suddenly occurred to me that Rocha must have been in one of the closed rooms with a woman. I cursed myself for being a fool and a coward not to have stayed at the place long enough to spot him. I motioned to Mingo for us to leave. I was so angry with myself I didn't notice the telephone on its table and collided with it. The table crashed to the floor, and as I tried to stop it all I did was burn my finger and help it on its way. The telephone made the loudest noise, taking an eternity as it skeetered across the floor and fell apart. Mingo and I held our breath in the darkness. There was a hurried noise in the lefthand room, and something in there seemed to fall to the ground as well. We stood stock still, but nothing happened. Perhaps Martha was opening the side window to call to the men in the car. I threw myself on the door and fell into the room. It was just as dark inside; someone bumped against a piece of furniture. I felt for the switch and turned on the light. Martha was standing in the middle of the room completely naked. She had knocked into a chair as she groped for her nightdress. Her long black hair hung down over small, firm breasts. She had a slender, milk-white body with gently roun-ded hips. Her mouth was open, but she couldn't bring herself to scream. I put a finger to my lips to beg her not to. Beside me, Mingo seemed to be in raptures. We stood in the doorway, carrying our shoes, without the faintest idea of what to say.

"Excuse us," Mingo finally stammered, unable to take his eyes off her.

Martha grabbed her nightdress, clutched it in front of her, and fearfully edged her way back to her bed. "What...what are you doing here?" she murmured.

I couldn't think of any excuse, so I told the truth. "We were looking for Rocha..."

She stared at us, on the verge of tears. She looked like a twelve-year-old, peeping over the top of her bedcover.

"Get out of here," she hissed. She didn't seem inclined to shout for help. She looked horrified and confused by Mingo's presence. His ear and his coat collar were covered in blood. It was no kind of face to wake up to.

"Please leave," she repeated, as though asking a great favour.

I turned and bumped into Mingo. As I was opening the door, one of my shoes fell out of my hand. Embarrassed, I bent to pick it up, and it was then that I saw the Cycles Club teeshirt on the floor. I scanned Martha's face. She looked guiltier than a cat caught with the last of the canary's feathers in its teeth.

"Where is he?" I asked.

She swallowed hard. "Who?"

"Don't pretend. Where's Rocha?"

She dug her teeth into her bottom lip, clutched her pillow, and began to cry. Behind me, Mingo made soothing noises.

"Get out," she screamed. "Get out of here!"

I went over to the bed, gripped her skinny shoulder, and shook her. "Don't shout! Do you want to wake the whole town?"

I felt an enormous pincer tightening around my right ankle.

"Get your hands off her!"

I'd forgotten all about him. His enormous head appeared from under the bed, his eyes darkened with rage. He tried to pull himself out, but with Martha sitting on top, he was kept prisoner by the bed-frame. He heaved, and the bed shot a yard across the room. I struggled free of his grip, and jumped out of reach. Martha gave a long sigh, buried her head in the pillow, and began to sob theatrically. Her tears redoubled Rocha's rage: he put his hands down on the floor, arched his back to lift the bed, and began to emerge like a cork from a bottle.

"You bastard!" he shouted.

His face was pressed against the floor, but he had managed to free his hairy back, at the cost of two long red weals.

"Don't be crazy," I said, in a last attempt to stop him. "Don't you see they're playing you for a fool?"

Martha sobbed again, and Rocha roared. He was wriggling his backside free, and in a moment would be entirely out from under the bed. I picked up the chair and held it above the back of his head.

"Move and I'll split your skull open," I warned him. Martha started in fear. Two teardrops and the remains of her make-up fell from her brown eyes and furrowed her cheeks. Mingo must have felt sorry for her, because he went over and patted her head. He wasn't exactly a reassuring sight, so Martha lashed out at him with the pillow. The tramp dropped his shoes, and crept back quietly into his corner. Rocha glanced up sideways at me to see whether I was capable of carrying out my threat. I put on the fiercest expression I could muster, planted my foot on his left shoulder, and pushed him down against the floor.

"Take back what you said," he muttered, less sure of himself.

"I'll take it back when you wake up to what's going on."

"I'll smash your face in," he growled, "I'll beat the daylights out of you."

He was straining to twist his head, to lift his purple, contorted face up at me. I carried on waving the chair about.

"Listen, will you? Our lawyer friend is a pimp...the fight has been fixed for Sepulveda, and..."

"It's all lies!" Martha jumped out of bed, pulling the sheet with her, and slapped my face twice. Then she began pummelling my chest in best television soap opera style. With the chair in my hands, I was powerless to stop her, and Mingo didn't seem ready to rush to my defence. Rocha seized his chance to struggle free. He was as naked

as a bear and twice as hairy. With his injured hand
he snatched the chair from me and flung it against
the wall, just above Mingo's head. The tramp
ducked, and was showered with bits of splintered
wood. The not-so-gentle giant grabbed me by the
neck, drew back his right fist, and was about to
punch, when Martha fell into his arms.

"This is terrible!" she wailed. Rocha stopped in
mid-air, and the muscles in his forearm relaxed.
His wild eyes filled with tenderness. He smiled in a
way I'd never seen in him before, put his right arm
round Martha's waist, and lifted her like a baby.
He slipped his other arm under her knees, and
crossed the room with her as though walking on
air. I would have dearly liked to leave on the spot,
but then why had we gone to so much trouble?

Mingo had no such doubts. He slid towards the
door, but didn't get that far; Rocha tripped him
up, and he fell against the wardrobe. Then Rocha
installed Martha on the bed with all the delicacy of
a gazelle, and kissed her on the forehead. Now it
was my turn. He came for me, choosing the spot to
hit me.

"Let me explain," I begged him, but he kept on
coming. I tried another tack: "A boxer shouldn't
hit people outside the ring."

I don't think he even took the trouble to listen.
He aimed a left at my liver, but I dodged and it
caught me on the back. I fell at Martha's feet, and
was sure I'd never breathe again. It was then we

all heard a noise outside.

"Papa!" Martha squeaked, then fell silent. The rest of us stood like statues.

"I'm going to talk to him," Rocha said at length, gazing at Martha. "After the fight we'll get married, that'll square it."

Things didn't seem that simple to me. If Aguila Bayo saw us all in Martha's room, he'd call out the whole regiment. I stood up and looked over at the window, hoping to beat a dignified retreat. The lawyer opened the front door, switched the hall light on, and said in a low voice, "It's cold outside, and you've been sitting there for hours...leave your guns here and we'll make some coffee."

My knees turned to jelly. I pushed the door to without making a sound. I was so nervous I couldn't locate the light switch, but I finally managed to turn the light off. Too late: Aguila Bayo had seen the reflection in the corridor and called out in what he must have thought was a tuneful voice: "Martha, my love?"

I took out my lighter and lit it. I found Martha's nightdress and passed it to her.

"Get out there," I said, as quietly as I could. "Go and tell him the first thing that comes into your head..."

"I'll talk to him," Rocha repeated, but this time his voice was an unenthusiastic whisper. I hushed him, and blew out the flame.

"Martha, are you there, my love?" the lawyer

insisted.

Martha jumped out of bed with surprising spirit and put on her nightdress. As I moved away from the door to flatten myself against the wall, I was sure she was going to give us away. She went out and immediately bumped into her father.

"Martha, why have you got the light on, my dear?"

He must have noticed the mess in the hall, because he went on to complain: "And what's this? What happened to the phone? I bet it was that animal..."

Rocha clicked his tongue at the description. To judge from the sounds, Aguila Bayo was picking up the pieces of the telephone.

"It was me, papa...I don't know how it happened..."

"All right, all right...let's see...the telephone is still working, no harm done...where's my kiss? Hmmm, what's that perfume in your hair?"

"What?...No..."

"What have you put on it?"

It must have been the lotion they had used on Rocha's hand.

"It's to lighten my hair," Martha said. "Are you with someone?"

"The boys guarding the house are in my study; we're going to have a coffee. Don't let them see you in your nightgown. Are you getting up now?"

"Can I have another half hour?"

"If you give me another kiss."

She did.

"Did Rocha go to bed early?"

"I think so. I haven't heard a sound from him all night." Her voice was studiedly casual.

"I'll wake him. It's six o'clock."

"How did you get on at the barracks?... Let him sleep a little longer, poor lamb."

"Fine, as usual. Perhaps he'd like a coffee with us."

"No, I've got a better idea. As soon as I'm dressed I'll go and buy some fresh pastries and then you can call him."

"All right, but we mustn't let him sleep all day. Off you go."

Martha came back into the room and switched on the light. She heaved a long sigh of relief, staring down at the floor. I was going over to say how sorry I was when there were two taps at the door. Mingo dodged behind the wardrobe, Rocha flung himself to the other side of the bed, and I flattened myself against the wall by the door. Martha opened it.

"Bring a good few croissants, will you?" Aguila Bayo said.

She must have nodded, because no more was said. Then she shut the door again. Mingo reappeared from his hiding-place, and Rocha scrambled to his feet. He hugged Martha, kissed her on the cheek, and began to caress her hair.

"I need to talk to you two," I said.

Rocha glowered at me. Before he could open his mouth I got in quickly.

"I want to apologise," I said, as gently as I could. "I was rude and showed no respect."

Rocha shrugged. A weary but satisfied look came into his eyes. He'd had a good night, and couldn't keep up his anger. "All right," he conceded. "Since you've apologised...did I hurt you?"

"I forgot it with the fright Aguila Bayo gave me. You have to get back to your room as quickly as possible."

"But how?"

He looked imploringly at Martha, as if she was bound to have the answer. She did.

"I'll get dressed and go to the kitchen to say hello to them. I'll make sure I shut the door, so you can get back into your room."

"What about them?" he jerked his head in our direction, only at that moment registering that Mingo was present. "What's that bum doing here?"

"He came to give me a helping hand."

"Thanks a lot. A real helping hand you two gave me, and no mistake."

"Why won't you believe me? The army's behind

108

Sepulveda..."

"I can fight him sitting down. I don't want to hear any more about it. Whose friend are you anyway, mine or Sepulveda's?"

He was getting angry again, and raised his voice.

"You know you're in no condition to fight. You've got one hand injured, and you haven't slept all night."

"The winner gets a crack at the championship. Go tell that to your friend," he said, trying to be ironic. Then he snapped, "Now you two turn round while Martha gets dressed."

"What about you?" Mingo asked.

Rocha looked down at himself in surprise, and blushed scarlet. "My clothes are in the other room," he said in a confused attempt at explanation.

The three of us turned our backs while Martha put her clothes on.

"Listen, Rocha," I insisted. "We've been walking all night to come and warn you. We even went to the..."

Mingo shot me a warning look, swivelling his eyes in Martha's direction.

"Well, we tried everywhere," I went on; "do you really think this is all a joke?"

"If I knock him out, they can't steal the fight, can they? What round would you like?"

Now he was poking fun at me. Martha came to comb her hair in front of the chest of drawers mirror. She put her hair into a long ponytail. Her high-necked blue dress made her look thinner, and once again I had the impression of a gawky adolescent. I couldn't say in front of her what I thought of Aguila Bayo, and I realised that if I insisted, Rocha would only think I had no faith in him. As if I was afraid that Sepulveda would still be on his feet at the end, and the judges would award him the fight.

"Don't you worry," Rocha said, squeezing my arm. "I know the score."

There was no way I could convince him. I looked over at Martha. I couldn't help feeling sorry for this scrap of a girl who was sitting on the edge of the bed putting her shoes on. I looked more closely at her room. On the bedside table were a bottle of eyedrops and a copy of *Nocturno* magazine open at the page where Rocha had surprised her. A case against the wall contained a few books, among them, I think, *The Count of Monte Cristo*, which I remembered reading myself once upon a time. A fake porcelain jewel case, a vase of fresh roses, and a picture of Aguila Bayo getting married to someone, all stood on the chest of drawers. Another photograph, stuck into the edge of the mirror, showed Martha aged 12 or 13, wearing an organdie dress, grinning, her hair in pigtails. A well-polished silver crucifix hung over her bed. Further along the wall was a small painting of pine trees in a snowy landscape. I was still making my inventory when she made a suggestion.

"You two could escape through the window."

Mingo opened it cautiously. Daylight flooded the yellow lamplight of the room. Rocha had discreetly put on his shorts and the Cycles Club teeshirt. Martha finished making the bed.

"Are you willing to help me out?" I asked Rocha.

He looked at me suspiciously.

"Meet me on the corner by the station two hours from now."

"What's the problem?"

"Those thugs are after me."

He looked surprised. This wasn't the moment to tell him the whole story. "Go to the police," he said.

"Will you be there or not?"

"You want me to defend you?"

"Right."

"How many of them are there?"

"I don't want you to fight them. If you're there, they won't lay a finger on me."

He swelled with pride. "You leave them to me."

"See you in two hours then," I winked at him, and was almost sure he responded.

Mingo picked up his shoes and jumped out first,

with an agility that surprised me. From the passageway, I could see Rocha, in his blue shorts and yellow teeshirt, put his arm round Martha's waist and kiss her on the neck. Then he shut the window in my face.

"It's years since I saw a woman naked," Mingo sighed.

CHAPTER ELEVEN

I finished my tenth *maté* while Mingo used the latrine he had made at the back of the waste lot, between two trees. It was a pit covered over with a plank and a slatted fruit box, which allowed him to sit in some comfort but can't have been much fun in winter. I got another pair of trousers out of the case Mingo had hidden for me, and put them on. I hung up my clothes to dry in the sun. At half past nine, Rocha got out of a taxi at the station entrance and looked around. Two kids recognised him and stopped to talk. He ruffled the smaller one's hair, and feinted a left hook to the other boy's head. Though they were still damp, I put my shoes on, got my jacket from the branch where I'd hung it, and crossed the street.

"Where'd you spring from?" he asked.

"Across the road, at a friend's house."

He searched, but seeing only the waste ground thought I must be joking.

"Mingo's," I said.

"Who's Mingo?"

"The guy with me earlier."

He crinkled his nose in disgust. He was even more exhausted than me, and that was saying a lot.

"Why are you always going around with that bum? You made me look like a fool."

A boy walked past with a bundle of newspapers. Rocha saw him, let him walk on five yards, then called him. He trotted back and sold Rocha *La Razon* from Buenos Aires. It was the previous afternoon's edition.

"Let's go to that bar. I have to talk to you."

"Where've the thugs got to? I'll soon sort them out for you."

"Come and have a coffee."

It was one of those places with a formica counter and tables. It was deserted, and the owner asked us what we wanted without stirring from behind his till. I ordered two coffees.

"So you're determined to fight?" We had sat down close to the door.

"You're not going to start that again, are you?"

I told him everything Mingo had told me.

"And you believe what a bum like that tells you?" he said, downcast, staring at the froth on his coffee.

"Even if it's not true, you have to admit that with no sleep and your hand injured, you don't stand much chance."

"I wouldn't fight someone like Monzon even on the telephone," he said, attempting a grin, "but I

114

can soon dump this guy."

"And if you don't?"

He shrugged, leaned on his elbows, and fixed me with his watery eyes, now circled with great purple lines. "Give me a cigarette."

I gave him one and asked the barman for another pack.

"And if you don't?" I insisted.

He was silent for a while, drawing on his cigarette.

"This is my last chance."

"You're not old."

"I'm 34. It's my last fling."

I drank my glass of water and studied the scar tissue on his face.

"This is it. Make or break."

"And afterwards?"

He began to cough. A hacking sound like a dog choking on a bone. He scraped his chair back and pulled out a crumpled handkerchief. The bar owner stared at him.

"You shouldn't smoke; sportsmen shouldn't smoke," he shouted from behind the counter, where he was making sandwiches. Rocha didn't hear him, or pretended not to. When the coughing subsided, he blew his nose and sat trying to catch his breath.

"You don't give up, do you?" he finally said.

The barman brought over my cigarettes and

seemed keen to join in the conversation; Rocha's glare made him change his mind, and he scurried off.

"OK," Rocha said, "now who is it that's got it in for you?"

I told him everything that had happened since he had moved to Aguila Bayo's.

"How come you looked for me in the whore-house? Who d'you take me for?"

"They might have forced you to go or something..."

"See? You think it's me who's taken for a ride, but in the end you're the one who needs me to pick up the pieces."

He shook his head indulgently and added, "What can I do for you?"

"Take me with you wherever you go. They won't dare touch me if I'm with you."

"Am I supposed to take you into the ring as well?"

"Yes."

He leaned back in amazement. "You're joking."

"No, I'm perfectly serious."

"What do you mean, in the ring?"

"As your manager, or your second, the guy who sponges your face at the end of each round."

"They'll give me one."

"Tell them not to, that I'm your manager."

It took a while for it to sink in that I was being

116

serious. He thought it over while he drank his coffee.

"You'd only throw in the towel," he said.

"You see? Even you don't believe you can win."

He shook his head, troubled.

"I don't mean it. Know how many fights I've had?"

"No."

It seemed he'd been in the game since primary school.

"A hundred and eighty-four. And I've never thrown in the towel. One guy wanted to once...know what I did to him?"

I was genuinely fascinated.

"I threw him, his bucket, sponge and everything out of the ring. I was disqualified for misconduct, but nobody tells me what to do."

"Not even Martha?"

He stared at me so intently that finally I lit a cigarette.

"I'm sorry," I said. "I didn't mean to stick my nose in where it doesn't belong."

"Where it doesn't belong?" He blew smoke into my face. "You even check out what we're doing in bed!"

"We didn't mean to... How was I to imagine that...?"

"Yeah, of course it's only tango singers who can pull the women, isn't it?"

"I didn't say that. But you must admit she was begging for it..."

He went crimson, threw the cigarette away, and stood up. "Say that again."

I pushed my chair back. "Calm down. I was only joking. Just to test your reactions..."

He sat down, relieved. "Don't try making any more jokes about Martha, you hear me?"

I nodded. We sat there for a while. Eventually, looking sheepish, he said, "I'll talk to her father after the fight - it'd only unsettle me before."

"Are you going to ask for her hand?" I took a strange pleasure in seeing him squirm.

"Well, she's a great kid...and I'm the first man she...the first, get it?"

"I get it. You're quick out of the corner all right."

He grinned mischievously. "Will you be best man?"

"Manager and best man?"

He hesitated, but in the end accepted: "Done." He stuck out his left thumb to clinch the deal. His hand was still swollen, and there was a livid blotch where they'd hit him on the old scar. "But you have to promise me one thing."

"What's that?"

"That after the fight you'll serenade Martha for me. Sing a couple of tangos under her window. Maybe we could do something together."

"Serenades are out of style."

I could just see Aguila Bayo and his friends in the car enjoying our performance.

"I know, but that makes it even better. It's not everyone who can bring along Andres Galvan to sing at his fiancée's window."

"Don't get me wrong, but I never..."

"You never...!" he guffawed. "Look at all the shit you get into for all the things you never do. Remember the autograph..."

I smiled resignedly, and brought the discussion to a close: "You win."

He beamed with pleasure, and began to day-dream about the hours following the fight.

"Listen," I said, "I'm going to take my first decision as your manager. Let's go back to the boardinghouse and sleep until a couple of hours before the fight, so we'll both be on form."

"But Aguila Bayo asked me to lunch."

"Phone from the boardinghouse and tell him you're eating with me. Better still, I'll call him, then he'll know I'm in your corner."

"Remember, I don't want any problems with him, so don't put your foot in it."

"Don't worry. To repay his kindness, invite him and Martha to dinner after the fight. Then when they go home to bed we can serenade them, OK?"

"Now there's an idea!" He was as beat as a fighting cock, and I was offering him a good excuse to go to bed. "If we'd met up earlier, I'd probably be champion by now."

He had a broad grin on his face. "Come on." He stood up. "I'll pay. We'll take a taxi, eh?"

The boardinghouse landlady gave us the same room. I asked her for the phone, looked Aguila Bayo's number up in the book, and prayed his phone was working. He didn't like what I had to say, and told me so. I slipped in a reminder that he still owed me my money and that I wanted it that night. I also told him Rocha and I would be leaving on the Monday train. Then I passed on the dinner invitation. He asked to speak to "Señor Rocha". I said Rocha was already asleep.

"But he slept all night," he protested. "He can't spend his whole life in bed."

"That's what he does before every fight. And tell Sepulveda to watch out: before he went to bed, Rocha smashed the wardrobe with his right."

I told the landlady we weren't to be disturbed, we were not in for any visitors. I asked her to wake us at seven, and to make sure there was hot water. Before I went back to our room, I gave her a fat tip.

Rocha was snoring away in the exact position he had flopped down. I undressed, picked up the newspaper, and lay on my bed. A small box on the sports page, despatched from Colonia Vela, previewed the fight, but the photograph was of Sepulveda. "The unbeaten local heavyweight, Mar-

120

cial Sepulveda, will take on the veteran Tony Rocha here on Sunday night. The winner of the contest in Colonia Vela will automatically become contender for the Argentine title, to be settled in a fight against Jorge Saldivar from Cordoba, scheduled for Luna Park in Buenos Aires next January. Rocha has won two, lost one and tied one of his last four fights. Sepulveda, aged 23, is unbeaten after 24 professional bouts, and has won the last seven by knockout."

I hid the paper. I was no boxing expert, but I'd seen a lot of fights from Gatica on. The problem was, I'd never seen Rocha. I recalled the question the station master had asked when I arrived. What Rocha had said that morning tended to confirm the idea that he was finished, or at least over the hill. I could think of only two cards in our favour: Martha, and Rocha's own pride. Martha probably wouldn't be at the ringside, so I had to arrange for him to see her beforehand. I mulled it over, then got up, put my trousers on, and asked the landlady for the phone again. The tip had brought out her friendly side. I had no idea how to explain to Aguila Bayo that I wanted to talk to his daughter. I asked the landlady to phone for me, and to make up a name to bring Martha on the line. She grumbled, but did it. I told Martha we'd come by for the bag at eight, and that Rocha would like to see her. She said all right in a cold voice, but with a hint of enthusiasm. I guessed her father must be standing next to her.

Back in our room, it took me a while to fall asleep. I couldn't help wondering whether the hand dangling from the bed beside me would be up to punching anything harder than a pillow.

CHAPTER TWELVE

It was three in the afternoon when they broke the door down. It was double locked, but they didn't bother to ask the landlady for her spare set of keys. I sat up with a start, and found four men pointing guns at me. Fatso and Gary Cooper were to the fore. Behind them were two swarthy characters who looked as solid and as friendly as a pair of tombstones. The fat guy slapped me so hard across the face with his right hand I was knocked clean out of bed. Rocha got up as though he wasn't sure if he was asleep or awake. One of the walking graveyards jabbed him in the chest with his machine gun and forced him to sit on the edge of his bed.

The blow hadn't really hurt me, but I saw everything covered in white dots, like a stained photograph.

"Get up, manager," Fatso growled.

I struggled to my feet.

"So you think you're cute, do you?"

I didn't reply. He seemed worked up, as if he was being tickled at an awkward moment. He left his machine gun on the chair where Rocha had dumped his clothes, and came at me. He pushed me up against the wall.

"A real smart ass, aren't we?"

He wasn't interested in my opinion. He slapped me again, but this time I blocked him with my arms. He didn't like that, and aimed a left to my forehead; the back of my head hit the wall, and I slid to the floor. He must have been wearing a ring, because blood spurted into my eye. Groggy as I was, the sound of splintering wood and glass brought me around. The thug who'd been covering Rocha had smashed the mirror and the door of the wardrobe with his back, and hung half inside the remains of the furniture. Rocha was standing on my bed, his head scraping the ceiling. Fatso scrambled for his gun, tripped over Gary Cooper, and shouted: "Don't shoot him! Don't shoot!"

Rocha jumped off the bed and advanced towards them. Gary Cooper brought up his machine gun, but Rocha didn't even notice. He grabbed the runt by his long hair, shook the breath out of him, then threw him out of the room exactly as he had dealt with Romero. Realising it was his turn next, the other thug decided to get in first. He slammed Rocha in the stomach with his gun butt, and the boxer doubled up in agony. He caught him with his right knee, and Rocha fell to the floor next to the bed, gasping for breath.

"That's enough," Fatso said. "Cool it, this one's

124

got to fight."

I was still on the floor, wiping away the blood with the corner of a sheet. The fat guy stood in front of me, kicked me absent-mindedly in the ankle, and spat.

"Manager!" he said. "Great idea. We'll meet again after the fight."

Sunny Sam fished his friend out of the debris and helped him stand up. He didn't seem to know what had hit him. Gary Cooper appeared in the doorway, hair smoothed down and his temper up, but the fat man restrained him: "Later, Beto, later."

Beto found a high-heeled boot he'd lost in the fracas and leaned on the doorframe to put it back on. Then he covered Rocha with his gun while the other two left. Fatso slung his machine gun over his shoulder, and felt in his pocket with his other hand. He threw something in my face. I recognised it at once.

"He won't be needing it any more," he said.

They all left. Mingo's hat, its band torn off, lay on the floor. I picked it up; it was still wet, and stank. I washed off my cut in the handbasin, and drank a glass of water. Rocha was sitting on the bed, rubbing his jaw.

"They didn't have it all their own way," he muttered. He hadn't really recovered yet.

"They've killed Mingo."

He looked up at me, but it was a while before it

sank in. "How do you know?"

I handed him the hat. He examined it inside and out, then dropped it on the bed.

"Are you sure? Why should they want to kill a hobo like him?"

"Why do you think they brought us the hat. As a present?"

He picked it up again, this time with more interest, and tried to smoothe it out. "Did he have any family?"

"No."

"We'll have to see to his funeral then."

He was solemn, as though suddenly moved. He laid the hat down, and began to force his shoes on.

"Why?" I said. "What's the point?"

He picked up his coat, looked for my jacket, and threw it onto my bed.

"He was your friend, wasn't he?" he said. "The least one friend can do for another is to light him a candle and throw a spadeful of earth on him when his time comes."

The taxi dropped us three blocks from Mingo's shack because the police were sealing off the roads for the parade. Rocha walked in front of me, and stealthily cut two roses from someone's garden. He halted at the waste lot, uncertain how to get in, intimidated by the weeds that spilled out onto the sidewalk. I showed him the path to the shack, and he went up to it with the flowers held out as though he'd been invited to dinner. Mingo's body

126

was swinging from the thick branch he'd used to support the hut roof. They had hanged Mingo with his own belt; his blue tongue lolled down on his beard. What I could see of his face was a ghastly white; his eyes staring down still had a terrified look in them.

"Holy shit," Rocha said, with all respect.

I dodged to one side, hoping to avoid Mingo's eyes, but his glaucous gaze followed me until I was right behind the body. His grey striped trousers were around his ankles; his raincoat had been pulled down to trap his arms. The box he kept the *maté* tea and sugar on had been knocked over and smashed as if someone had given it a kick. Among the mess of things on the floor were the butts of two candles. I put the box by the body, asked Rocha to take the weight, and clambered up to untie the belt. The corpse fell stiff onto Rocha's shoulders; he laid it carefully out on the floor. The raincoat gaped open, showing the burns on Mingo's legs and balls, where the hair was singed. Rocha found a half-burned candle to put with the two butts. He placed them on the ground, level with Mingo's chest, and asked for my lighter. He lit three feeble flames, crossed himself, and stayed there on his knees. We could hear a band in the distance. It was five in the afternoon, and the church bells rang out. One by one, the candles flickered and died, until the only light left was the faint sunlight that filtered in through a hole in the sacking. I drew back the rag curtain at the entrance and emerged into the waste ground. I took a deep breath, and stared up at the sky where a few white clouds were floating. A couple with two children walked by in the street; the kids gawped at me then made some kind of joke. The band was playing a triumphal march. Rocha squeezed out of the hut doorway, came over to me head down, and laid a hand on my shoulder.

"Tomorrow with the money from the fight, we can buy a coffin," he said.

We walked in silence through the weeds. I was remembering the crickets, the aircraft, Mingo's voice, his gestures.

Drawn by the music, people were heading for the town centre. I signalled to Rocha for us to take the opposite direction. A couple of blocks further on, we found a bar with iron tables and chairs, and ordered two beers. Rocha was gloomy, and I sat there staring at the passers-by. I sipped at my beer, trying to discover some taste to it.

"What's Sepulveda like?" I asked, for the sake of something to say.

Rocha wrinkled his snout. "A bigmouthed kid," he said.

"Why?"

"Everybody reckons they're a big shot at the start."

He was fiddling with the bottle top, and occasionally took a peanut from the dish in front of us. The other tables were empty. Rocha pulled up another chair and stretched a leg out on it. Then, as though absent-mindedly, he said, "Why do you want to be my manager if you don't believe in me? For what you can make out of it?"

"Sure, so when you win we can go on together to the world championship."

"I'm serious," he said, smiling. "Do you believe in me or don't you?"

"How d'you feel after the beating?"

"What beating?"

"The one just now."

"Oh, that was nothing," he punched his own jaw. "It's made of iron, feel it, go on..."

He could have done with a shave.

"How often have you been knocked out?"

"Me?" he whistled smugly. "Twice, and only when I was a kid. Never since. Listen, once I was knocked down by a car and I didn't even pass out. I got up and walked to the hospital, with two ribs broken. What d'you make of that?"

"You may find yourself doing it again..."

He laughed out loud, sure of his professional skill. "Don't be a fool," he said. "You know I'll wipe the floor with him. Can you imagine how furious they'll be after the fight? Beating the local boy is like winning against the police chief's horse."

"Well then?"

He smiled and spread his palms. "I'd give anything to see Martha."

"You're going to see her."

His eyes opened as round as footballs. "When?"

"At eight. We're going to get your bag from Aguila Bayo's, and she'll be waiting for you there. I spoke to her this morning."

He squeezed my arm so hard I couldn't help wondering how Martha's ribs felt. "You're a real pal."

He stared at me. His sadness had passed like a shower of rain.

"What about you..." he began.

He finally got his nerve up. "Apart from singing...apart from your records and things..."

He pressed his two forefingers together and winked over them at me.

"No, there's no one waiting for me, if that's what you want to know."

He was a bit put out at my reply. "Nobody at all?"

"Well, there is a shady lady who sometimes remembers me when she's drunk."

He was indignant. He shook his head sorrowfully, and tried to console me: "Some women!"

He downed his beer in one. He was warming to his subject.

"But you've got family...brothers and sisters..."

I glanced down at my watch. It was six o'clock,

and the sun was deserting the town.

"We can talk on the train. It's a long stretch."

"I'll sleep the whole way. The noise of a train always sends me to sleep. Want another beer?"

"No. Aren't you hungry?"

"I could manage a steak. I always have a snack before a fight..."

I asked the boy who had served us, and we went inside the bar. We ate chops with salad, and after the coffee I began to revive. By now, Rocha was in a good mood, and told me that whenever he won a fight his grandma would make him special meat pasties. When we reached Buenos Aires, he said he'd get her to make a few dozen of them, and he'd invite Martha and me over. Then he asked if I thought he should call for a minute's silence in Mingo's honour at the stadium.

CHAPTER THIRTEEN

At five minutes to eight Rocha eagerly rang Aguila Bayo's front doorbell. A recently pressed blue and white Argentine flag hung from the balcony, and the sidewalk had been swept. We heard hurried footsteps coming to the door. Rocha smoothed down his pullover and rehearsed his best smile. The door opened about six inches, and a short, fat, black-haired woman poked her glasses into the gap. She was a female version of the lawyer. The sparkle in Rocha's eyes was snuffed out like birthday candles.

"Is Miss Martha at home?" he managed to blurt out.

"She went to the function," the woman said, pursing her lips as if she could have said a lot more.

Rocha swallowed and asked faintly, "What function?"

"The gala function."

"Ah," Rocha murmured, staring at her. The silence grew heavier and heavier, until she pushed the door to, so that only half of her glasses remained visible. "Well then," she said.

Seeing the door closing in his face, Rocha made one last desperate attempt: "Where is it?"

"What?" the woman asked from behind the slit.

"The...the function."

"In the theatre. Who shall I say called?"

"Rocha."

"Oh, so you're Rocha? Why didn't you say so before?"

A glimmer of hope flitted across his face.

"Wait there a minute," the woman said, leaving the door open wide enough for us to watch her walking away, swinging hips as broad as a table top.

Rocha glanced at me, and began wringing his hands until the knuckles shone white. He turned his back for a second, then said, embarrassed: "Don't get me wrong, but d'you think you could take a walk?"

He hopped about on the kerb trying to conceal his shame at asking me to leave him on his own. I was going to walk to the street corner and back, but I saw the woman reappearing along the corridor.

"This was left for you," she said, holding out Rocha's bag. He made no attempt to take it, so I had to go to her help, taking it and dropping it on the sidewalk.

"What about her?" he struggled with the words.

"Martha, I mean."

"She's gone to the function with her father. ...So you're the boxer?"

Rocha nodded. "In the theatre you said?"

"Good luck for tonight," she said, flashing a toothy smile that still glinted as she shut the door.

Rocha stood staring at the door, then as he stepped back, almost fell over the bag I'd left on the ground. He lashed out with his foot, swore, and when he looked up his eyes met mine.

"What the fuck are you staring at?" he snarled.

I didn't answer. He punched the palm of his left hand a few times, walked around in a circle once or twice, then sat at the kerb with his back to me.

"It's only natural," I told him, "she had to go with her father, didn't she?"

He found a stick and drew shapes in the dust at the edge of the road.

"We have to be at the boxing stadium by nine," I reminded him.

Rocha jumped up as nimbly as a featherweight, and though it was such a brief gesture, it gave me the vague hope that I hadn't given enough credit to what he was capable of when his pride was at stake.

"Wait for me there," he said, crossing the road.

I picked up his bag and trotted after him. "Where are you going?" I shouted.

"To find her."

"Are you crazy?"

He didn't answer. We hurried along the empty sidewalk. When we reached the corner, I grasped his shoulder as firmly as I could. He dragged me along a couple of yards, but finally came to a halt.

"She said she'd wait for me, didn't she? So why didn't she wait?"

"I've already told you. Her father must have taken her with him."

"I'm going to talk to him," he said, striding off.

"You're nuts. How can you talk to him at a function..."

"I'm going to ask for her hand."

I tugged at his arm again, but he pushed me off and walked on another couple of yards. I ran to get level with him.

"How can you do that? You're really crazy...after the fight..."

"No, now. I don't like keeping things hidden...I'll tell her father we're engaged, and that'll be that..."

My patience was exhausted. I bawled at him: "You dumb ape! You can't ask for her hand at a function like that!"

He flung me against the wall. I staggered, lost my cigarette, my legs doubled under me, and I fell flat on the ground. I dropped Rocha's bag, and it rolled into the road. I had banged my knee, and the palm of my left hand burned as though I'd scalded myself. Two men walking on the other side of the road paused for a second, then carried on, still staring at us. I felt ridiculous and furious. Rocha stopped five yards further on and called out harshly:

"What the shit is a gala function anyway?"

I struggled to my feet. My knee was throbbing, and I could put hardly any weight on my leg. "Fuck off and leave me alone, will you?"

He came back and looked down at me puzzled, as though unable to understand that I could be so hurt by such a small thing.

"Come on, it's nothing. I caught you off balance, that's all."

I began cursing him again, but he knelt down and started to dust off my trousers.

"There, it's nothing," he said, as though soothing a child, "it's only a scratch."

He straightened, scooped up the cigarette, and puffed at it while watching me try to walk again.

"What is a gala function?" he repeated.

"It can be a concert, or something like that," I explained.

He let out a sigh. He reached over and stuck the cigarette back between my lips. Then he went to recover his bag, and said, condescendingly: "All right, you can come with me if you like."

"You think I'm chasing you so you'll let me go with you? Do you have any idea how stupid you are? I was trying to stop you making a fool of yourself, to stop them laughing in your face."

"Who's going to laugh?"

"All the people there."

"But I mean it sincerely. I love her..."

"That's got nothing to do with it."

"Hurry up, we don't have much time."

For half a block I hobbled after him, but as I warmed up the pain became bearable. I calculated that at the last moment, when he saw what a gala function was like, Rocha would change his mind. Outside the theatre, posters stuck on two wooden easels announced the performance by Romero and his guitarist friends. The foyer was deserted, and as we pushed through the glass doors we could hear a fragment of what sounded like a Vivaldi concerto. The music checked Rocha's charge; he began to tiptoe in. He jerked his head at me to indicate I was to follow him. He opened the back door to the hall just as a violin was soaring in search of paradise. We stood still until our eyes had become used to the darkness. The place was full. Rocha was gaping at the stage. On it were a dozen musicians with a bald conductor who was waving his baton and moving energetically to the music. When the whole orchestra began to play, Rocha turned to me and showed how marvellous he thought they were. Then he started off down the aisle. By the time he'd taken five steps he'd disappeared in the dark. His strides made the wooden floorboards creak despite the carpet. I could see the audience in the back rows turning their heads and could imagine their indignant protests. Vivaldi died away in a last lament that was intended as ecstasy, then the musicians relaxed. The audience applauded fit to burst. The conductor bowed deeply to acknowledge the applause. Captain Suarez appeared on stage in a shiny uniform, went up to the conductor, shook hands, and offered congratulations which were accepted with a nod of the head. The applause reached fever pitch, and suddenly all the lights came on.

Halfway down the aisle, Rocha kept switching his gaze between the audience, who by now had all risen to their feet, and the stage. He looked lost. Caught in a crossfire, scared he might be stealing some applause that wasn't his by right, he turned back up the passageway. After a few steps he apparently realised the musicians might think he was leaving in disgust, not sharing the general delight. So he turned to face the stage and also began to clap. He walked backwards to where I was standing, doing his best to beat an honourable retreat. Someone shouted "Bravo", and others took up the call. A man in evening dress close by me shouted for an encore; his wife echoed him with a loud braying.

Aguila Bayo climbed on to the stage, shook hands with the conductor and then with Captain Suarez, and stepped forward, lifting his arms to call for silence. He was quite a sight in evening dress: this time he was wearing a huge black bow tie which looked like a gigantic fly that had somehow landed on his shirt front.

Taking advantage of the sense of anticipation created by the lawyer's appearance, Rocha backed up a few more steps, and when he collided with his bag, realised he'd made it to safety.

"It wasn't the right moment," he commented, still clapping loudly. The rest of the audience had quietened down to listen to Aguila Bayo, so Rocha's last handclaps rang out in the uneasy silence as the lawyer began: "I am honoured..."

He had to start again.

"I am honoured," he repeated, in a gentle, almost effeminate voice, "to have helped organise this magnificent occasion which the nation's armed forces are offering for the people of Colonia Vela. I say I am honoured, ladies and gentlemen, and trust you won't think me immodest. I am honoured to have discovered in Lieutenant Colonel Heindenberg Vargas an accomplished and sensitive musician as well as a model officer. A man who took up arms in our nation's darkest hour and who, now that peace and respect have been restored, takes up his simple baton to regale us with such a sublime *Four Seasons* that I am sure the immortal Vivaldi himself would have wished to be present to enjoy the splendid interpretation offered by the chamber orchestra of the Fifth Airborne Cavalry Regiment."

More wild applause. I glanced at my watch, hoping perhaps Rocha had forgotten about his fight. He was clapping too, but this time kept a close eye on the others to make sure he stopped in time. On the lighted stage, Aguila Bayo halfheartedly called for silence. The applause eventually died away.

"But it is Captain Suarez who is the true inspiration behind this gala function for you, the leading citizens of Colonia Vela, and the other entertainments to be put on for the common, labouring folk." He smiled and spread his arms wide, "As you well know, some people prefer the clash of fists to the gentler pleasures of the ear, and so Colonia Vela today hosts a boxing contest, and will soon host the world champion, whose talent has developed thanks to the discipline and fortitude instilled in him by the gentlemen of the Argentine army. I believe, ladies and gentlemen, that although we cannot be with him later, our First Lieutenant Marcial Sepulveda, who this evening is taking on an opponent from the capital, deserves a round of applause from us."

Fresh clapping. Sepulveda, in his best uniform, climbed up onto the stage. Rocha was thunderstruck.

"He's the one I'm fighting, isn't he?" he asked.

I said he was. He went on gaping at the stage in disbelief.

"Aren't they going to call me up too?" he

muttered.

"It doesn't look like it."

"They usually present both boxers, don't they?"

"That's in the ring. It seems you'll be taking on the whole army, friend."

He stared at me. His tiny eyes registered astonishment, but also a glimmer of reason. For the first time, I think he realised what he was in for that evening. The audience had finished applauding. Captain Suarez lifted Sepulveda's right arm high in the air, while Aguila Bayo, trying to maintain a semblance of calm, shouted: "Good luck, champion!"

At six foot six, Sepulveda was a couple of inches shorter than Rocha, but his body looked more streamlined and supple. His fair hair was cropped in a military crewcut, and his uniform made him look like a movie idol. He stepped forward discreetly to the front of the stage to speak:

"Captain, fellow officers, ladies and gentlemen: you as citizens, and the army to which I have the honour of belonging, have jointly entrusted me with a mission on a front which for a number of reasons has until now been left in the hands of civilian personnel. The sporting front. That is where I am called on to fight, and all my colleagues fight alongside me. Just as, at the cost of great sacrifice, we have been victorious in battle, now we will triumph in peace. Put your trust in me as you have always trusted in your nation's soldiers. I will bring the Argentine title to Colonia Vela, and soon after that, the world crown. I will be champion, and with me the real Argentina will be champion too."

The audience had started to applaud again when Rocha burst out with: "Champion my arse!"

The spell was broken. There was a tense silence, with all faces turning towards Rocha. In the front rows, filled with Suarez's cronies, the curiosity was more veiled, as if they were all waiting for instructions on how to react. On stage, the captain himself stood poised, waiting for Sepulveda to continue. Rocha strode five yards up the aisle and halted. He could see everyone craning their necks to see who he was. He raised his arm and pointed at the lieutenant.

"You and how many others reckon to beat me, eh, rosebud?"

With that one word, so unlike his usual range of expressions, he completely won the audience over. I think everyone in the hall forgot about Sepulveda and turned their attention to Rocha. Everyone but the captain, that is - he was still standing stiffly to attention, stoically resisting this barbarian invasion. He thundered: "Continue with your speech, Lieutenant!"

Sepulveda, who was staring at Rocha, nearly jumped out of his skin. He pulled himself together, stole another sideways glance at the boxer, then went on, "Yes, Captain, sir." Then he stammered:

"An army which...which...seeks to..."

"That's it, stoolpigeon," Rocha said, reaching unsuspected levels of irony, "lick your corporal's arse, go on..."

The loss of rank Rocha inflicted on the captain caused widespread indignation; one person cried "throw him out"; another wanted "the guard called"; a woman scowled "he's drunk". Captain Suarez turned to consider Rocha for the first time. I couldn't see his face, but it took him a good minute to recognise Rocha and to mutter something to the musicians. In full evening wear, they left their instruments on the floor and felt for something rather different they were all carrying between their jackets and shirts.

Aguila Bayo stepped in.

"Friends," he said, "we are all aware of the verbal abuse that is planned and carried out prior to any important boxing match, and we often read in the press of the unpleasant antics of people such as Ali. I am afraid that our pugilistic friend from the capital, who until this moment had shown such admirable behaviour here in Colonia Vela, is now resorting to the deplorable tactic of slander and gratuitous insults in order to place First Lieutenant Sepulveda at a psychological disadvantage before their fight this evening. While all of us are willing to take his reckless language with a dose of good humour, none of us can allow his calumnies to stain the honour of our nation's

143

armed forces..."

"I couldn't give a fuck about the armed forces or this shit-hole of a town!" Rocha screamed, and few if any could hear his voice breaking with emotion. He swept round, taking us all in with his gaze. The audience, the musicians, the Captain, me. His eyes were glistening, but I could have sworn he was not crying. For the first time I wished with all my heart that he would fight, that he'd climb into the ring and demolish this smug lieutenant, that he'd cut him to ribbons, shatter the captain's self-assurance, destroy the fickle dreams of the lawyer and these upright citizens of Colonia Vela. Perhaps he sensed what I was thinking, because he kept staring in my direction even as a dozen soldiers ran down the other aisle and across the front of the stage. Now the audience was busy following the military operations. They watched intently as the recruits took up position without any fuss at each corner of the hall, guns at the ready. But they all knew Rocha was on his own. Three soldiers went up to him.

He didn't resist, but he didn't help either. He let himself be pulled, pushed, threatened with the guns. Then all of a sudden he halted, shook off the soldiers like troublesome wasps, and shouted with all his might:

"Martha!"

Then a second time: "Martha!"

All the Marthas in the audience must have

stirred uneasily, but none of them answered his call.

"Martha! I love you, Martha!"

On stage the conductor and the musicians hastily put away their service revolvers and picked up their instruments. On behalf of the army, Aguila Bayo apologised for the interruption. His voice betrayed both surprise and sorrow. Not towards Rocha, though: the lawyer was peering down at the front row, where a woman had begun to sob.

CHAPTER FOURTEEN

The orchestra struck up an encore of *Spring*. Aguila Bayo, the captain, and two men went out to the foyer. People were whispering, leaning over, passing messages. When Martha ran up the aisle where I was standing, everyone looked around. Rocha had destroyed her future in the town, devastated her dreams of finery and lace. I moved slightly in front of the curtain at the back of the darkened hall, and blocked her path. She stopped in surprise. She was clutching a damp handkerchief, and looked so dejected I felt sorry for her. At another time, in other circumstances, she and Rocha might have made just another couple.

"Why?" she asked, her voice quavering. "Why?"

She started to cry again. I took her hand and put my arm around her. Her cold tears ran down my neck. We stood like that for a while, with Vivaldi in the background, until her sobbing abated.

"He...he was the first...," she stopped crying and said, talking to herself, "he was so gentle, I never...why did he do this to me?"

I thought about it, but couldn't think of a proper reply. "He felt robbed," I said.

She cried some more, dabbed her eyes with her handkerchief, and murmured: "What will they do to him?"

The foyer door opened and Captain Suarez, the lawyer, and the two other men reappeared. As they passed us, I overheard Aguila Bayo mutter, "He's finished anyway." He walked on a couple of steps, then turned and looked in our direction. He came up slowly, trying hard to make out who exactly it was in the darkness. Recognising Martha, he grabbed her by the arm and hissed:

"Get back to your seat."

She struggled free of his grip.

"No, I'm going home. I'm taking a taxi home."

"Aren't you satisfied with what you've done to me already?" His anger came welling up from deep inside; a black anger. "Go fix your face and return to your seat."

It was an order.

"Papa, I didn't mean to..."

"We can talk at home."

Martha hesitated, but in the end obeyed.

"It was all Rocha's fault," I said.

The lawyer turned to me, but I couldn't see his face properly in the shadows.

"His fault? Do you think we don't know who put the idea in his head? That dumbbell isn't capable of tying his own shoelaces."

"What do you mean?"

"That it was you who put him up to it, you who tried to stop the fight by telling him a load of nonsense."

"Well, that's that. With Rocha in jail, there's no fight."

He was silent for a moment. When he did speak, he sounded amused. "In jail? Why would we put him in jail?"

"For insulting the armed forces. You could have him shot for that."

He laughed silently, so as not to disturb the orchestra.

"You take us for fools, don't you, Galvan?" He wiped his face with a handkerchief. "A lot of people took us for fools, and soon learned otherwise."

"What are you going to do with me?"

"With you? Some of the boys want to rough you up a little, that's all. Don't overestimate your importance - you're as finished as Rocha is. They don't make heroes like Gatica and Gardel anymore, my friend."

He swaggered back to his seat in the front row, his tiny body swaying to and fro like a plump black seal.

I picked up the bag and went out into the street. The army jeeps were parked outside, packed with soldiers. I crossed to the square. Lit

148

by a distant lamp, Rocha's silhouette was just visible under a mimosa bush. He was sitting on a wooden bench, head in his hands. I stood looking at him. I remembered a film where the hero, beaten and humiliated, drew enough strength from his love for a girl to destroy all his rivals in one last assertion of dignity. I lit a cigarette and went over. Rocha didn't budge, or even glance up at me.

"Is it time?" he asked.

I told him it was.

"You bring the bag?"

I put it next to him on the bench. A sudden clap of thunder made me jump. Then a lightning flash lit the square. Rocha opened his bag and pulled out a pair of tattered gloves. He gazed at them.

"I bought them when I was eighteen. The first gloves are sacred."

"It's getting late."

He lifted his head. "Do you believe in me?"

"Are you going to wear those gloves?"

"If they'll let me..."

"They'll let you."

He didn't want to take a taxi. I asked where the Union and Progress Club was, and we set off across the square and then down a cobbled street. A bunch of kids were walking along the opposite side of the street, heading for the fight. We'd walked two blocks when Rocha asked me, "Was she there?"

"Yes."

"You saw her?'

"I talked to her."

"You talked to her?" He stopped in his tracks.

"Just a couple of minutes, before her father arrived."

"Was she mad at me?"

"Why should she be?"

"I dunno...I blew my top...the soldier boy got me wound up."

"The first lieutenant, you mean," I reminded him.

"Yeah, the lieutenant. What did Martha say?"

"That she'd have liked to go to the fight to be near you."

I sensed he was blushing. He smiled and shook his head.

"Is that what she said?"

"Sure. And she was pleased you didn't let them get away with treating you like that."

"What a kid, eh!" he said, smiling to himself.

When we reached the next corner he ostentatiously put his fists up and hit me with a left jab to the arm. I raised my guard and we began to shadow box. The passers-by stared as if we were madmen, but it was too dark for us to be recognised. I couldn't get past his arms, and he cuffed my ears a couple of times as he circled around me, feinting and laughing. When I ran out

150

of breath I dropped my hands and leaned against the wall, panting.

"Well, what d'you think?" Rocha asked.

The lights of the stadium shone out from the next block.

"OK," I said, "but try not to stand so square on." I put my fists up and showed him, my left shoulder well forward. "Like this, see?"

He stared at me in amazement. Then he burst out laughing. "What a joke! You'd have died of starvation as a manager!"

"And above all, remember you can do it. Have faith in yourself. Imagine..."

I realised I was going too far, and walked on.

"Imagine what?" he shouted from behind me.

"Imagine Martha is at the ringside."

He didn't reply, and we walked the rest of the way in silence.

There was a long line outside the gate. Some people recognised Rocha and booed him. One fat guy shouted, "He'll leave your face like a squashed tomato." We pushed our way through the crowd, with Rocha complaining that there was no special entrance for the boxers.

The ring had been set up in the open air on a basketball court. Four rickety stands had been erected, like the ones used to watch parades from. There seemed to be more people in the stadium than in the whole town.

Our dressing room measured about ten feet square. One wall was covered with soccer posters. Another had a poster of Susana Gimenez emerging from the sea, and a metal locker with no key. Rocha threw his bag on the massage table, which might have been big enough for a middleweight, but was nowhere near his size. A short guy, dressed in white from head to tennis shoes, brought us towels and a bar of soap.

"Give me the gloves and start getting changed," I told Rocha. He rummaged in the bag and handed them over. They weighed a ton. "Are you sure you want to use them? You won't be able to lift your arms."

"I've never been beaten in them," he said, taking off his trousers and throwing them on a chair.

I was at the door when he whistled to me. I turned around.

"Take my dough and my watch. And take your jacket off. Whoever saw a manager in a suit?"

For a moment I thought he must be joking. He was standing by the table in his underpants, the temperamental champion, freezing me with his glare. I took my jacket off and hung it from the back of the other chair, carefully keeping it clear of the filthy floor.

"Your tie as well," he insisted.

I took it off.

"While you're at it, roll your sleeves up, to

152

prove you're on the job. If you want to be my second, don't show me up."

He threw me a towel.

"And don't smoke in the changing room."

I tossed the towel over my shoulder and went out into the corridor. I asked for the referee's room, and knocked at the door. He was medium height, with greying black hair, and sported a fifties' style pencil moustache.

"I'm Rocha's second," I explained. "Galvan, good to meet you." I held out my hand.

He smiled and shook it.

"My pleasure. We've met before, haven't we? How is the old slugger?"

"Being a bit difficult. He wants to use the gloves he first started with," I held them out. "Is that OK with you?"

He examined them, weighed each one in his hand, then gave them back. "He's crazy."

"Do him this favour. It's his last fight."

"His last?" He seemed surprised. "But if he wins he's got a crack at the title in Buenos Aires."

"If he wins."

He gave me a solemn look and wound his watch. "You can never tell."

"So?"

"They'll fall apart by round two and I'll have to replace them. Anyway, Sepulveda has to agree."

"What if he doesn't mind?"

He shrugged. I said thanks, and set off down the corridor to what appeared to be the local fighter's room. I knocked, but there was too much noise going on inside for anyone to hear me. I pushed the door open, but a voice called out "Not now". I said who I was, there was a brief exchange, and I was allowed in.

First Lieutenant Marcial Sepulveda lay stretched out on a long padded table. He was relaxed, and hardly deigned to open an eye to check who his visitor was. I couldn't have meant much to him, because he immediately shut it again. A short guy with a pug nose wearing a teeshirt with the name of his protégé across it was massaging one of Sepulveda's legs. An army recruit asked if I was Galvan and smiled warmly at me. I went up to Sepulveda and thrust the gloves under his nose.

"Is it OK for Rocha to use these?"

He opened his eyes lethargically like a cat, seeming not to understand. Then he took them, swung to a sitting position, and feigned surprise. "He wants to use these? Hey, Shorty, take a look at this."

He threw him the gloves. The pug caught one; the other landed on the floor. The soldier picked it up for me.

"Poor kid. We can lend him a proper pair," the man called Shorty said.

"No, it's not that. He wants to use this pair. They bring him luck."

154

"That's his look-out."

He handed me back the glove, holding it by the end of the lace and swinging it in front of my face.

"Is he really washed up?" Sepulveda asked.

"Washed up?"

"The old man. He can hardly stand, can he?"

"Don't count on it."

"No, come on. Don't let him take a beating." He was genuinely concerned. "When he's had it, pack it in, will you?"

"Worry about yourself, you may get a nasty surprise."

"I'm not bullshitting. Take care of him."

I wished him well, and as I was leaving grabbed a bottle of rubdown oil. His second stared at me but said nothing. In the corridor I bumped into two boxers who were in the supporting bouts. They tapped each other on the back of the neck. The one going out had his hair carefully combed, and did knee bends on the spot. The other one had puffy eyebrows and a split bottom lip. Either he had been soaked or he'd been sweating far too much. I heard him say "on points", but his face betrayed no emotion.

When I got back to Rocha's room I found him shuffling around, punching the air. He was a replica, older and on a much bigger scale, of the two I had just passed in the corridor.

"Been to the movies?" he growled.

"I was checking out the gloves. You can use them."

"No kidding?"

I handed them to him.

"Shit, you'd have made a great manager! What shall I call you? The Maestro, the Wizard?"

Someone knocked at the door and called round. "Get ready, boys," the voice said, slamming it to.

"Wrap the tapes," Rocha said. "Know how to?"

I did the best I could. The bandages had once been white, and still had two blue lines near the edge. His left hand was almost as swollen, but by this time that was a mere detail. The door opened again, and the same guy poked his head in.

"Time to go, boys."

"I'll be there," Rocha barked.

"Get a move on, the last fight was a knockout. The crowd's really warmed up." He snapped his fingers like a whiplash, with relish. This time he left the door open. Rocha draped the largest towel over his shoulders. I was about to go out when he grabbed me by the arm.

"Listen, there's something I want to tell you." He gave me the gloves, which he'd tied together by the laces. "You're new to this, and could let anything get to you. But listen - unless I tell you to, don't throw any nonsense into the ring, OK?"

I looked at him blankly.

"I mean the towel, the sponge, or anything like

156

that, OK?"

"OK."

He winked and strode out ahead of me.

CHAPTER FIFTEEN

The boos started almost before we left the dressing room. Ignoring the noise, Rocha held his head up and trotted to the ring. He slipped through the ropes almost elegantly and raised a nonchalant arm. Then he came over to the corner. I climbed the wooden steps and looked around. It was a more impressive sight than I had imagined. At my performances, I was used to a far more respectful and appreciative audience.

The referee climbed slowly into the ring and leaned against the ropes, an old hand at the game. A photographer who must have been from the local paper took a couple of pictures with a flash and then waited for Sepulveda. The guy in white who'd brought us the towels and soap arrived with a microphone. There was still some booing, but it was only sporadic. Then everyone in the crowd got to their feet and began chanting: "Se-pul-ve-da, Se-pul-ve-da". Someone sounded a klaxon that must have been heard for five miles around.

Rocha waited for Sepulveda in the middle of the ring, without going to help him through the ropes. The first lieutenant came up with his hand outstretched, but Rocha's only response was a tap on the forearm. The applause died down, and the crowd began to settle in the seats at the ringside or on the boards of the stands. Another sound filled the air. I looked up and saw a helicopter hovering over the stadium, its red lights flashing. The master of ceremonies announced the fight in flowery language that was lost amid the helicopter noise and the renewed shouting as soon as he mentioned Sepulveda's name. The referee gave a speech to the two boxers, neither of whom paid him the slightest attention, but stood there twitching like epileptics. Rocha refused a second time to acknowledge his opponent, and strode back to his corner. I held his gloves while he pushed in his fists, then tied them as tight as I could. I tried to put his gumshield in, but he turned his face away.

"Not yet. You do that at the bell."

I was so keyed up by the fight I had forgotten everything that had happened before. The bell rang sharply. Rocha bit on his gumshield and went out to the centre of the ring. As I climbed down the wooden stairs I heard the first roar from the crowd. I turned to see Sepulveda bouncing gently off the ropes, looking at Rocha's chest with his guard down. So we had thrown the first punch, and the sight of Rocha standing there steady and calm gave me fresh hope. The crowd began to chorus "Se-pul-ve-da" again, and the lieutenant poked out two probing straight lefts. Rocha blocked them with ease and on the bell hit Sepulveda with a good short right to the midriff.

"He's not bad," Rocha said while I wiped his face with the towel.

He was breathing hard, but I had no idea whether this was normal at the end of the first round or not.

Rocha was the clear winner of the second round. Sepulveda didn't know what to make of him, and though he moved around smoothly enough he took three punches to the head that wiped off the relaxed expression he'd started with. Rocha left himself wide open as he pressed forward, but whenever Sepulveda was measuring him for a punch, he attacked so furiously that the lieutenant was forced either to cover up or to backpedal without launching a blow.

After a few cheers and hoots of the horn, the crowd had gone silent. For the third round, Rocha did without the gumshield, and went out breathing through his open mouth. It was then the rain started. It was the same clinging drizzle as the night before, and the crowd forgot the fight for a minute while they put up umbrellas or draped newspapers over their heads. I couldn't take my eyes off the boxers, except when I glanced up and saw the helicopter's red lights flashing even closer above us. The sound of its whirring rotors made my hair stand on end. Rocha paused in confusion, and Sepulveda slammed a left into his face. Rocha lurched forward, got him in a clinch, then wrestled him into our corner. Over the lieutenant's shoulder I could see Rocha's nose had started to bleed. Locked together, they tried to punch the back of each other's neck until the referee pulled them apart, shouting something that was drowned out by the noise from the helicopter. As he stepped back, Rocha took another punch on the chin, but he pulled his head back in time to soften the blow. The crowd went wild though, and a man in a pinstripe suit who looked like a bank manager leapt from his front row seat and started thumping the canvas close to me.

"You've got him!" he shrieked. "The bread basket! Hit him again in the bread basket!"

Sepulveda had got inside Rocha's guard and was giving him a hard time. Rocha couldn't force him into a clinch, and took a short jab to the body that would have poleaxed a horse; then the lieutenant stepped back, steadied, and smashed Rocha's nose with a devastating straight right. Rocha's knees wobbled, he staggered back and almost sat on the second rope. Sepulveda was in no hurry, and began to show what a clever boxer he was. Keeping his distance and staying out of trouble, he hit Rocha with a combination punch that Rocha could only block untidily. He took the left on the ear and must have been stunned, because when the bell rang for the end of the

161

round he walked uncertainly back to the corner.

"Don't stand so square on," I told him. "Jab with your left to keep him away. Is your hand OK?"

"Go take a jump," he replied, and spat into the bucket. His nose was a bloody mess, and all his face was red. He rinsed out his mouth, and looked up at the helicopter, which had lifted slightly higher in the sky.

"What shit awful weather," he growled while I was dabbing at his nose with a wad of cotton. He let me get on with it, and as he went out to the centre of the ring, he glanced up again at the sky. I climbed down the steps, thinking I should ask for something to stop the bleeding. When I reached the ground and turned to look, I found myself level with Sepulveda's startled face. He was on his knees, one arm hanging through the second rope. He began to lug himself up. I thought for a moment the referee was coming over to begin the count, but instead he helped him up. It was only a slip; the referee borrowed my towel to wipe off his gloves. Then he slid his feet across the canvas to test if it was fit to continue. He put on a worried look for all to see, and leaned over to talk to someone at the ringside. The man who looked like a bank manager had got to his feet again, and was waving to attract Sepulveda's attention.

"He's finished," he shouted. "Go for the bread basket."

"Get it over with, Marcial, it's raining," some-body called out behind me.

Rocha seemed to have got his second wind. The break and the rain helped revive him. Eventually, the referee called the two men to the centre of the ring, made them touch gloves, and Sulpeveda took a short step backwards, slapping his gloves together. In that split second, God knows how, Rocha caught him with a whiplash right cross. Sepulveda fell on the spot like a toppled tree. I shouted something like "Rocha, you did it!" while the referee pushed him into the neutral corner. Sepulveda had a vacant look in his glassy eyes, like an old man who'd lost his spectacles. He was trying to haul himself up by the rope as the referee began to count, too slowly for my liking, struggling to make himself heard above the steady roar of the helicopter. With a great effort, Sepulveda made it to his feet, but his legs wouldn't obey him, and he was teetering like a bowling pin. The referee counted to eight and rubbed his gloves on his trousers. Rocha was on him: he hit out blindly, and Sepulveda bounced against the ropes, defenceless. End of the round.

"Got him," Rocha said, blowing like a pressure cooker. "One more punch and he's a goner."

"Stay calm. Pick your shots, don't lose your head. Nice and steady."

Two men had climbed into the ring and were mopping up the water with floor cloths. The

163

canvas was a slippery mudbath. In the other corner, Sepulveda's second was fanning him with the towel, his head bobbing as he furiously shouted instructions.

"Don't worry, you're way ahead on points," I told Rocha as he rushed out at Sepulveda, who was only just getting up from his stool.

All of a sudden, the noise of the helicopter engine became a deafening roar. It circled the stadium, dropped to a hundred feet above our heads, and the wind from the rotorblades tore umbrellas and newspapers from the crowd's hands, sending them scattering while people shouted in confusion and tried to escape. The spectators in the stand opposite me rushed to both sides, while down by the ringside everyone suddenly forgot the fight and dived for cover. Two rows of seats tipped back, and the people were falling all over each other until the helicopter rose high enough for everyone to be able to stand up and peer into the sky. Rocha, Sepulveda and the referee did the same whenever a clinch gave them the chance. All three had their hair blown about by the downblast of air, but didn't seem to realise what had actually happened. The helicopter rose higher and higher and moved off until it had completely disappeared. In the silence it left behind, all that could be heard was the thud of the boxers' gloves, their rasping breathing, and the sound of Rocha clearing his nose wherever and whenever he could. The two of them were like ridiculous dancers in the centre of the ring. Sepulveda was trailing a sheet of newspaper from his right foot, and I suddenly realised it would be hard for Rocha to finish him off. Only a perfect punch, as lucky as the previous one, could end the fight. Which meant that Rocha would have to win by points even if the judges didn't like what they wrote on their scorecards.

At the end of the round, Rocha came back to the corner still looking up into the night sky. I pushed out the stool and he flopped onto it.

"What the fuck was all that?" he said, blowing his nose partly into the bucket and partly all over my shirt.

"The helicopter," I told him, and only then remembered to run my hand through my hair to smoothe it down.

He peered up again at the sky, where a thin rain was still falling.

"Did it beat it?" he said, spitting on to the canvas. "Thank God, I'd had a bellyful of that noise." He turned to me and said apologetically, "I couldn't concentrate."

I nodded understandingly.

"We're ahead on points. Keep jabbing with your left, don't let him get in close."

He turned to me again, smiling. I dried his face for him, then repeated the instructions, though I wasn't too sure they were the same ones I'd given a moment before. The bell rang, silencing the hum of the crowd. Sepulveda came charging out of his corner. They'd obviously been giving him a talking to, and he wanted to narrow the gap in points. He looked refreshed but worried. Rocha took a step back and hit him with a straight right to the nose which kept him off for a while. Rocha was full of surprises. He seemed cool, in charge of the fight. He clinched Sepulveda twice to avoid problems, then pushed him off so strongly he slipped on the soaking canvas. For a moment I thought Rocha had everything planned: the lead he had on points, his opponent's nervousness, the wet ring. Towards the end of the round, Sepulveda hit him with a left to the solar plexus which even knocked the wind out of me, but Rocha tied him up, waltzed him around a few seconds, and when the bell went, came back to the corner with a spring in his step.

"Give me a bit of a massage, but don't show everyone you're doing it," he said, glancing down at his right side.

I rubbed his back and then, more energetically, his sore ribs until he whistled and motioned for me to stop.

"We've got him where we want him," he said. It was the first time he'd included me in.

The next round was a bad one for Rocha. He slipped at the start, and Sepulveda caught him with a left that put him down. It was only a glancing blow, and Rocha was up at once, as if it had been an accident, but the referee completed the mandatory eight-count and dried off his gloves. By now he was as filthy as Sepulveda, with his shorts and one arm smeared with mud. The lace of his righthand glove had come undone and hung down like a bloody rag. He was trying to get away from Sepulveda the whole time, and I shouted to the referee for him to retie the lace, hoping Rocha could win a breather from Sepulveda's furious two-handed attack. I wasn't sure any more if we were still ahead on points. I calculated Rocha needed to be at least three points clear or the local judges would call it a draw. There were three rounds to go.

Rocha was hunched over trying to hold on to the lieutenant's waist, and eventually butted him in the stomach. Sepulveda protested loudly to the referee, but he told him to get on with the fight. Sepulveda punched angrily and hit Rocha on the back of his neck with such force he fell forward on his knees. He was still clutching Sepulveda's legs, and flailed wildly at his thighs. I thought he mustn't have realised he was on the canvas, and reckoned he was punching Sepulveda's back in a clinch. A few moments later he pulled, and Sepulveda fell flat on his back, like a piano from a fourth storey window, spattering all of us within a ten-yard radius with mud. The referee ran to help Rocha to his feet. Sepulveda was already up, even more furious, swearing at Rocha and waving long arms dripping with mud. Rocha was completely groggy and leaned over the ropes gasping for breath. The referee got a towel from Sepulveda's corner and began to wipe both boxers like a fussy mother. Sepulveda's second had climbed up to the ropes and was screaming like a madman; I realised I had to do the same. I ran over to join in and climbed up to the ring.

"That was a rabbit punch, ref!" I shouted, throwing in a few insults for good measure, though they couldn't in any way match those Shorty was coming out with.

The referee paid no attention to either of us. When he'd finished wiping the boxers dry he told me and Shorty to get down off the ring, and waved his arms theatrically to restart the boxing. The bell rang and Rocha headed back to the corner.

He was still groggy. I threw water in his face with the sponge, but his only reaction was to run his tongue over his lips. I pulled at his shorts to get him to sit on the stool, and when I saw his face close to I knew he'd had it. I squeezed the sponge on his neck, and he grinned.

"He's on his way out," he said.

"What about you?"

He didn't reply. I squeezed more water onto his neck. The bell for the next round came too soon, and Rocha took one of the worst beatings I've ever seen. After the fourth punch to the face he dropped his guard and began to dance around Sepulveda blindly, as if he was in control of the ring. The lieutenant took aim and hit him with his

168

heavy artillery. Rocha rocked back from each blow like a punchball. His feet skidded, he tottered, but he would not fall. Sepulveda lined him up with his left then hit him with his right just as if it was a practice session with the bag.

His second was shrieking, "To the head, Marcial, to the head!" and Marcial hit Rocha in the face. "Now the body," Shorty cried, and Marcial obliged by socking Rocha in the midriff. I looked at my watch. It was a long time to the bell. I picked up the sponge, and had it ready in my hand to throw. Suddenly it seemed far too tiny a thing to halt Sepulveda's cold fury. The bank manager was on his feet again in the front row and copied each of Sepulveda's punches with dramatic gestures of his own. A fat guy with his coat wrapped around his head to keep the rain off came up and shouted in my ear: "What are you waiting for, you murderer, stop the fight!"

A kind of stupid compassion prevented me throwing in the sponge. A right cross sent Rocha sprawling against the ropes. He looked down at me. His face was a mass of gory flesh; his mouth was open as if in a constant yawn, and his chest was heaving five times a second. His knees bent and wobbled like rubber, but they were still far enough apart to keep him on his feet.

His face was turned towards me. It looked yellow now, but perhaps that was because of the lighting; I didn't think he could recognise me any more; I must simply be another hazy and menacing face. But just as I was about to throw the sponge (was I going to throw it?) he moved his head slowly from side to side, and the referee put up an arm and led Sepulveda off to the opposite corner. He walked slowly back to Rocha, who, like a blind rhinoceros, was still ducking and feinting, amazed not to feel any more blows. The referee began his count, and Rocha nodded, saying yes to everything that was happening around him. The referee reached eight, and shouted to ask if he could carry on. Rocha steadied himself, and put up his fists. Sepulveda's assault continued for another twenty seconds. He even hit him twice after the bell.

It took Rocha a while to work out which way to go, then he used the rope to find the route back to his corner. I helped him sit down, then tipped a bottle of water over his head.

"That's enough," I said. "I'm going to stop the fight."

He looked at me through swollen eyelids, and cuffed me on the chin with his glove.

"Leave it to me," he said. "You don't understand a thing."

"I'm going to stop the fight."

He could scarcely take a breath, but when he spoke the anger was clear enough.

"You were the one who asked to come here. If you want to chicken out now, you can go."

He stood up, hitched his shorts, and waited for

the bell on his feet. Then he went straight out to the centre of the ring. Sepulveda threw his right, but Rocha brushed it away and ducked underneath the left, which he'd seen coming. He hit out with a couple of quick, aimless punches, but it was too late. Sepulveda caught him with a one-two to the face, then a crunching left to the body. As if in slow motion, Rocha began to sit down, looking for all the world as though he was controlling and positioning his body as it fell like a superb stage actor. Before he reached the canvas, Sepulveda hit him again with a left hook to the chin that sent up such a shower of mud and blood his glove seemed to have burst open. This punch jerked Rocha straight, and he fell stiff to the canvas, out for the count. His face stared up at the sky; his right arm dangled limply as if it had been smashed to pieces. The referee counted slowly to ten and out! But as far as I could see he could have carried on to twenty thousand without Rocha stirring. Sepulveda raised his gloves in triumph, and his second hung from his neck with delight. Half the crowd was in the ring before me. I soaked the sponge and went to help Rocha. People were stepping over his inert body as if he had never existed. They all wanted to touch Sepulveda, who had finally managed to force a way through to his corner.

I squeezed out the sponge on Rocha's face. The only signs of movement came from his eyelids and a vague flapping of his right arm. A kid, sparring with a friend, trod on Rocha's left hand, stumbled,

171

and stared shamefacedly at the pair of us.

I got Rocha to a sitting position, but his head lolled against my arm. His lips moved, then he closed his eyes, sunk deep in puffy brows and cheekbones. When I shook him, his jaw dropped to show a bright red tongue in a mouth full of bloody froth. I pressed my face against his and tried with all my strength to lift him to his feet. A man in a plastic raincoat bumped into me; Rocha's body fell from my grasp and thumped flat again onto the canvas. I knelt over him and put my ear to his chest. His heart was racing.

"Don't be scared," he said, barely audibly. His eyes were still shut, and he didn't seem in the mood for a speech. Someone knelt beside me and took his pulse.

"This boy's in a bad way," he said.

I got up and began to push my way through the people left in the ring. Sepulveda and his group were disappearing down the gangway. I shoved a couple more kids against the ropes and shouted out. Suddenly I realised nobody else was making a noise, that everyone was quiet, staring at us without moving a muscle, as if they had suddenly run into a funeral procession. And the rain still came down.

CHAPTER SIXTEEN

We laid him out on the back seat of a car and began to inch our way through the crowd. The people leaving the stadium mixed with all those who had been waiting outside in the street to hear the fight result. From doorways, windows and flat roofs, young and old applauded the procession of cars celebrating Sepulveda's victory. Everyone was sounding their horns, and my curses were lost in the general euphoria. Youngsters drummed triumphantly on their car doors; some had tied shirts and handkerchiefs to their aerials and windshield wipers. Somewhere in the distance a siren started up. Flares shot into the sky over by the army barracks, bathing the town in an eerie white light that slowly faded. We spent half an hour creeping forward at walking pace, without Rocha being aware of a thing. When we reached a service station at the first corner, the driver steered his way through the pumps and came out in another, less congested street. His hand pressed on the horn, he put his foot down and within two minutes we were driving up to the hospital. The front entrance lay beyond a pretty, well-tended garden.

A beefy redhead in a white coat was outside getting a breath of fresh air, smoking a leisurely cigarette. As we were getting out of the car, he shouted, "No admissions today. Come back tomorrow."

When I opened the back door to the car, Rocha's feet slid out to the ground. The guy who'd brought us tugged roughly at Rocha's ankles until he was lying flat on the paving stones. Then he jumped in behind the wheel and sped off before I could thank him. The orderly strolled over and peered at Rocha without bothering to kneel down.

"Go get him a stretcher," I said.

"How long has he been like this?"

"Over half an hour."

"Some beating he took," he said, whistling.

He dragged himself into the hospital, taking his time, and re-emerged with a trolley. We grabbed Rocha's arms and legs and lifted him onto it. The orderly made as if to throw away his cigarette, thought better of it, and instead balanced it on the edge of the trolley, between Rocha's legs. He signalled him with his chin: "What round was he knocked out in?"

I started to push the trolley. He followed close behind, and in the entrance hall rescued his cigarette.

"We'll put an ice pack on him and he'll come round."

"Call a doctor."

He looked at me as if I was from Mars.

"A doctor? Where am I supposed to find one?"

"Isn't there one on call?"

He shrugged to show how sorry he was. I opened the first door I came to, and found an empty examining room. When I turned around, the redheaded orderly was shaking his head at me.

"Don't do that to me, you hear?" he said, coming over menacingly. "Do you want me to throw you out?" he hissed. But then his tone softened.

"You're from Buenos Aires, aren't you? Me too." He jabbed himself in the chest. "I'm a conscript. I look older because I got a deferment. I study law for six years, then they send me to this shit-hole to wipe all the patients' arses. What d'you think of that?"

"Listen," I said forcefully, "this man may die. You have to find a doctor."

He bent over Rocha, and patted him on the cheek. "The doctor went to watch the fight." His face was suddenly solemn, "There's no sense of responsibility."

Rocha's mouth hung open, and a gurgling sound came from somewhere deep in his chest.

"Bring the ice," I said.

"If there is any."

I gave him some money. He looked at it, then stuffed it in his trouser pocket.

"For smokes," he said, and sauntered off to fetch the ice.

While he was gone I opened the other doors in the corridor. All the rooms were empty. I phoned Aguila Bayo from the office. Martha answered.

"I have to talk to your father."

"He's not in," she said, sounding crushed, "he's not back yet."

There was a silence that was too long for my liking. Eventually she asked: "How did the fight end?"

"Sepulveda won."

She sighed. She didn't seem to want to talk much. "Is Rocha with you?"

I told her he was, and she asked me to put him on. I said he was having a shower and that he'd call her the next morning. She didn't say anything. She must have felt abandoned, because before I hung up she started blubbering again.

I called the switchboard to see if they could find me a doctor. The operator explained there were only two in town, and that one of them should have been at the hospital. The other didn't answer his phone. I went back to Rocha. The orderly had left the ice pack on his head and wandered off again. I looked for a blanket, but had to make do with a sheet. I smacked his cheeks gently, and put my ear against his muddy chest until I could make out faint heartbeats.

Outside, the celebrations continued. The fireworks had finished, but the night was still filled with the sound of firecrackers and car horns. Somebody shouted Sepulveda's name over the loudspeakers, and promised there'd soon be an interview with the winner. I paced the hall, smoking and wondering what on earth I could do. A Citroën convertible with the top down rolled across the gravel path and came to a halt by the hospital entrance. A twenty-five year old with the look of a nightbird got out and walked wearily to the door. He gave me a brief nod and started to take his jacket off. When he saw Rocha on the stretcher, he went over and stared at him as though it was a crate of cabbages.

"I thought Furlari had seen to him," he said.

"Nobody's seen to him. He's been like this over an hour."

Reluctantly, he prised open Rocha's eyelids. Then he took his pulse, checking his watch, and listened to his chest.

"Are you a relative?" he asked.

"A friend. He doesn't have any relatives here."

"Aha. He needs a tracheotomy to help him breathe."

We stared at each other for a few moments, as if unsure which of us was going to do the job.

"I'll have to get the theatre ready," he said at length, offering me a cigarette. I tried to convey some urgency with my worried look, and he sauntered away to find the orderly and the nurse.

177

The three of them vanished down the corridor, then half an hour later the orderly came to fetch Rocha. He had brightened up, and winked at me as he wheeled the big fellow away.

"They're going to make a nice hole in him," he said, pointing to his own throat.

A dark-haired nurse appeared and told me to wait outside or to go for a walk. I went into the office and called Aguila Bayo again. This time he answered. I explained what had happened, and said I thought he should transfer Rocha to Buenos Aires straightaway. He didn't reply.

"They could take him in an ambulance," I said.

"Take him?" he sounded put out. "Really, Galvan, it can't be that serious. We can do everything there is to be done for him here. And we have to take the doctor's opinion into account. He'll be as good as new in the morning."

"If he isn't a whole lot worse."

"Don't always look on the black side. We'd only be making fools of ourselves if we took him to Buenos Aires, and it wouldn't do any good anyway. If he's no better tomorrow we can transfer him to the army hospital...Was it a good fight?"

"I reckon you ought to come here. I'd like you to see Rocha and talk to the doctor. I don't trust him all that much."

"Doctor Mancinelli? But he's first-rate! Don't get so worked up about this. I'll pop in tomorrow morning."

"Bring Martha with you."

"Martha? What on earth for? It would only upset her, poor thing."

"If Rocha comes around, he might want to see her."

His voice hardened.

"Why should he want to see Martha?"

"Well, he thinks very highly of her."

"And we think highly of him too. He's a grand kid."

I hung up. After a while the doctor reappeared to tell me he had put Rocha in the intensive care ward. He said I could have a quick look and then should go and get some sleep.

He was naked underneath a sheet. His body seemed a little straighter and more presentable. A long plastic tube led from his throat to an oxygen cylinder. He looked peaceful enough, except that the tube sticking out of his throat made him look terribly ill. I whispered to him, but the nurse warned me not to make any noise. At the end of the room was an old man lying very still with needles in his arms and legs who was sleeping or dying. I sat for a few minutes until I was told to go. I had a word with the orderly, reminding him of the money I'd given him, and he let me lie down in a tiny room where the only furniture was a low, filthy bed and a peeling cream-coloured table. I dozed off; when I woke it was four in the morning. A car braked at the hospital entrance, then I heard its doors slamming and orders being shouted. I peeped out. The green Ford Falcon was outside, and my old friend Fatso was the one shouting orders, still clutching his machine gun. His companions helped out a guy who moaned constantly, and looked in a bad way.

"Get a move on, shitface!" Fatso shouted at the doctor, who was helping lift the wounded man onto the stretcher.

I shut the door and sat there with the light out. People were running up and down the corridors for about an hour, then everything was quiet again. The car pulled away some time after six, with daylight already streaming in through the skylight of my room. I went out and half tiptoed along the corridor. The redheaded orderly was flat out in the emergency ward. I went to the room where they'd left Rocha. The nurse was asleep on a stretcher; I kept a close watch on her as I squeezed past.

Rocha wasn't in the bed. In his place was a man who I guessed was the one they'd brought from the Ford Falcon. He had also had a tracheotomy, and his chest was bandaged. He looked up at me, and I nodded. He replied with a groan that must have hurt, because he immediately grimaced. By the light of day the ward looked like a huge desolate barracks room. I leant closer to ask him if he knew where they had taken the man who had been in the bed before him. He winced as he lifted his right hand a few inches, then made a thumbs down sign.

I stood there for minutes in the gloom, watching the light struggling to force its way in through the grimy plate-glass. I looked at my watch, perhaps with the intention of giving substance to that particular moment, to have a precise minute to recall whenever I found the hands of my watch in that same position in the future. I went to find the nurse and shook her awake. She sat up without even blinking.

"Where is he?" I asked her.

"Opposite, in the general ward."

I crossed the corridor and opened the door. There were a dozen beds in two rows, with a couple of yards between each bed. They all had someone asleep in them, except for the furthest one, where an aged woman was groaning to herself like a scratched record, sure in the knowledge that nobody would come to help. Rocha, a sheet pulled up under his chin, was lying in a bed under a slowly rotating ceiling fan. His face was purple, and his hair was still streaked with mud. His jaw gaped open again, and his nostrils were caked with blood. I pulled down the sheet a little. In place of the oxygen tube there was a gauze bandage, held in place by adhesive tape that had traces of blood on it. His breathing was a faint whistle. I lifted one of his eyelids, but there wasn't enough light to make out anything more than a dull, dark mass. I left the room to find the nurse again. She had gone back to sleep, so this time I shook her arm.

"Where's the doctor?"

"Sleeping."

"Where?"

She must have seen I was in no mood for argument because she pointed straightaway to a door next to the operating theatre. The doctor was lying on an untidy bed; on the metal bedside table were a half-empty bottle of orange juice and an ashtray where he'd stubbed out an almost complete cigarette. I poked his leg, and he gave a start, then opened his eyes.

"What's the matter?"

"Why did you take him off the oxygen?"

"Who?"

"The boxer. Why did you take him off it?"

He swung his legs down and sat up on the bed. He rescued the cigarette from the ashtray and lit it with a match.

"There's only one cannula."

"What's that?"

"For the tracheotomy. We've only got one."

"But he had it, didn't he?"

"Yes, but the other guy needed it more." He shrugged and yawned. I grabbed him by the shirt and shook him.

"You bastard! Put him back on it!"

"What's with you?" he said, pushing me off.

"Who's the doctor around here anyway? The guy's had it, it won't make any difference one way or the other."

"What d'you mean?"

He sat staring at a spot on the floor. His cigarette had gone out, so he felt for the matches again.

"Everybody's got it in for me tonight. ...What d'you want from me, miracles?"

"Put him back on the machine. It's his by right: he was already using it."

He sighed bitterly and stroked his jaw. "Go tell that to the guard." There was a challenging edge to his weary voice.

"What guard?"

"The cop outside. Go on, give it a try."

I went to the door.

"Hey," he called after me. "Gently does it. I don't want to have to see to you as well."

I walked along to the room where the orderly was sleeping. On the other side of the corridor a door opened behind me. Gary Cooper peered cautiously out. His eyes had dark rings round them.

"Hey, what brings you here, Golden Voice?"

For a few seconds I was paralysed with fright. He'd taken his boots off and was no taller than a broom handle, but he was still carrying his machine gun, and a revolver bulged at his belt.

"What a night, eh?" He sighed as if we were close buddies.

I was still rooted to the spot in the corridor. I couldn't say a word.

"What's wrong with you?" he said. "Not still mad at us, are you?"

"What are you doing here?" I asked.

"You're still sore, aren't you?"

I said nothing, but kept on staring at him.

"They left me as lookout. Everyone else is living it up and I have to spend the night in the hospital. Too bad, ain't it?"

"Why here in the hospital?"

"Orders from the chief. One of the boys got hurt."

He opened the door wide. He left the machine gun propped against the wall, and took a few steps as if looking for something. Then he grabbed hold of a metal table, shook it until all the bottles on it fell off onto the bed, and stood it in the middle of the room.

"How about a game of cards? I'll wake the medic and the other guy and the four of us can play."

"I have to go."

"Go on..."

"Rocha's here."

"I know."

"I'm taking him with me. There's a morning

train isn't there?"

"The milk train. It takes forever. You'd better wait till tonight."

I shook my head and walked off to the general ward.

"Hey!"

I stopped outside the door and looked back at him.

"You two aren't really mad at us, are you? Orders is orders, you know."

There was more light in the ward. I found a trolley and wheeled it next to Rocha's bed. I tried to lift him onto it, but couldn't. I was going to need Gary Cooper's help. None of the others would have agreed to my taking Rocha out of the hospital. I went to fetch Gary.

"You're nuts," he said.

"He'll die if I don't get him to Buenos Aires."

He thought about it for a while, staring with regret at the table he'd pulled out for the game. "I can't leave my post."

"Just for a minute."

Suddenly his face lit up. "You can sign your autograph! Remember? Your signature! The chief will be green with envy!"

"All right."

He ducked back into the room, searched for a notebook in the table drawers and in a cupboard, found one and tore a sheet out. He handed me a pen. He was as pleased as if he'd won the lottery.

"Go on, put: to Beto Sayago, with affection from his friend...no, wait, put with brotherly affection from...that sounds better. And with a nice clear signature so everyone can read it, eh?"

I laid the piece of paper on the table and wrote the dedication. He grabbed the sheet, folded it as if it were more valuable than a check, and carefully stowed it in his shirt pocket.

"Where is he?" he said.

We sweated for ten minutes to get his trousers and jacket on, and lift him onto the trolley. Beto did all he could, and was even concerned about Rocha's condition. Afterwards he advised me to be sure I was out of town before Fatso saw the autograph.

"If anybody asks, say you spoke to me and the doctor."

"I'll call a taxi."

"A taxi? Not even the fire engines are getting through tonight. We had to blockade the centre at two this morning to make people go home. They were all crazy after the fight, the whole town was in the streets celebrating. That's why I said you should stay for a game of cards and leave this evening." He looked across at Rocha. "He's out anyway."

I said no again, and found myself forced to shake hands with him. He said thanks for the autograph and came with me to the front door. I had a hard time forcing the trolley along the gravel path. I had to push as hard as I could, and at the same time make sure Rocha didn't fall off. His body dangled over all four sides of the trolley, and his feet stuck out over the front almost to his knees. The sheet and blanket I'd covered him with kept slipping off, so I had to stop every minute to pull them back. The train was due in fifty minutes, and I had to cross the whole town to reach the station. The sidewalks were too bumpy, and I would have had to lift and lower the trolley at each street corner, so I carried on pushing him up the middle of the road. The town was completely deserted; the only sound was birdsong. I stopped every couple of blocks to catch my breath. I was worried that Rocha had only a thin blanket over him; I touched his arm - it was as cold and hard as butter from the fridge. I took off my jacket and spread it over his top half. I wasn't as anxious as I had been at first, but instead felt a deep sense of pity for this pig-headed fool who had refused to accept that his defeat was pre-ordained. Who knows, perhaps he was right: there had been a split second when victory was possible, within his reach, but he hadn't been able to grasp it. A single blow could have entirely altered this absurd story we were caught up in, surrounded by an indifferent town where nobody even opened a door to say goodbye, thanks a lot for spilling your guts for our entertainment. Maybe I should have asked for the fight to be called off because of the rain. Or maybe I should have thrown in the sponge when I had it in my hand and Rocha looked down at me in a last, stupidly heroic gesture. By now I'd reached the square, still struggling with the ramshackle trolley, where Rocha lay stiff as a statue, unable to share my pondering. I wondered if he was feeling any pain.

A dog that had been sniffing at the San Martin monument came and barked at us, followed by another two out of the trees. The first, a black puppy with a stub tail, jumped up twice and snatched away the blanket covering Rocha. I had to chase it for several yards before I could recover the blanket, which by now was filthy from being trailed along the ground. The other two dogs, a pair of huge, dirty mongrels, thought this was great fun, and barked furiously at my antics. When I finally got rid of the puppy, they ran after him, growling and nipping at his flanks.

We went past the theatre. As well as the two boards announcing the previous evening's concert there were several large, new photos of Romero and his accompanists, hatless in smart black suits. They all had fresh haircuts, and the streaks of white I'd noticed in Romero's hair the night he came to our room had been carefully dyed out. The corner bar was shut, but inside somebody was busy laying out the tables and chairs.

We were going back up the avenue that had brought us to the centre of town two days earlier, when Rocha had run after me and asked if I was here to earn a bit of dough as well. I was exhausted, and had to stop for longer each time to recover and dry off my perspiration. For the last two blocks I had to wrestle the trolley along, because it kept veering sideways, one of its wheels completely buckled. Before crossing to the station I looked over at Mingo's shack in the waste lot. I remembered that with the money from the fight Rocha had promised to buy a coffin to bury him in. I wondered if he was still inside, stretched out on the floor as we had left him, or if someone had taken away his body before it stank out the whole town.

The station master was standing in the middle of the platform, in the same black suit, hands in his trouser pockets. His hair had been freshly slicked back, and the inevitable cigarette drooped from his lips. He told me he'd been to the fight, that Rocha had been grand in the opening rounds but then had obviously tired and that Sepulveda should have knocked him out sooner. He wouldn't hear of the idea that Rocha had ever been ahead on points.

"In your shoes, I'd have thrown in the towel much earlier," he said.

He called over a man who was stacking some parcels, and the two of them helped me deposit Rocha on a bench in the waiting room. He stared at Rocha for a while, but contained his curiosity.

Then he said he'd never seen a knockout like it, and refused to charge for our tickets. He had two blue forms made out justifying our free journey in second class, and said how sorry he was the train didn't have any sleeping cars and took eight hours to reach Buenos Aires.

We had to struggle to get the big fellow onto the train and into a window seat where there was no risk of his toppling into the aisle whenever the train swayed. The compartment was almost empty; the other few passengers were asleep. I sat opposite Rocha in the seat of a man who agreed to change over to the other side of the compartment. I tucked the blanket around Rocha, and laid his head back against the rest.

As the train pulled out, the station master waved a brief goodbye, then disappeared into his office. The sun had risen, and dazzled me until the train rounded a bend and settled to a steady rhythm. I could see the whorehouse in the distance, standing alone in the middle of the fields, and suddenly felt everything had happened a long, long time ago. I was trying to conjure up some of the images in my mind when the guard arrived to check our tickets. I put my hand in my jacket pocket and felt the wallet Rocha had handed me before the fight. The guard punched the blue forms I'd given him and moved on without comment.

I looked everywhere for some sign of Rocha's

address. I had his watch, the wallet, and a bunch of keys. The wallet contained a few banknotes, a photo of an old woman with a cat in her arms, a lucky bus ticket, and a dirty, crumpled ID card. No address or telephone number. I wound the watch and put it on my wrist. The date on its dial corresponded to the one I'd seen on his identity card. I took it out again and looked for the birth date. Rocha was thirty-five that morning. I glanced across at him; the tape protecting the hole in his throat had come undone. I leaned over and stuck it back, taking care not to press too hard. The man who'd given up his seat couldn't take his eyes off us. In the end, he took a can of beer out of his bag and waved it at me. I shook my head, though my throat was dry as dust. Then he asked me what had happened to my friend.